COSTIGAN'S NEEDLE

Jerry Sohl

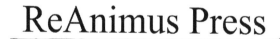

ReAnimus Press

Breathing Life into Great Books

ReAnimus Press
1100 Johnson Road #16-143
Golden, CO 80402
www.ReAnimus.com

ISBN-13: 978-1494304348

First ReAnimus Press print edition: November, 2013

10 9 8 7 6 5 4 3 2 1

For Jean

Part One: Discovery

1

His welcome home was snow. January snow, powder dry and cold. He saw it from his taxi and he hated it.

It was Chicago snow and Devan Traylor knew it well. Like Chicago, it would be big. From the feel of it he knew it was the kind of snow that came through keyholes and brought the cold with it and deposited a token drift on the floor in front of the door, the kind of weather that called all available men from the city yards to fight the drifts and keep the streets open.

He had never felt as furious with the snow as he did now, because he had been called back from Florida, summoned by a woman who insisted that something big had gone wrong. The call had come to the beach house where he and Beverly and the kids were starting a vacation that had been three years in the making.

Miss Treat had hinted there was something unusual in the wind. Had the gang at Inland Electronics deliberately waited until he was out of the way to do something? It did not seem possible. He knew them all too well. Yet he thought he knew Beatrice Treat and, when she called, her voice was taut and edged with caution and she said she couldn't risk telling him anything over the phone. That just wasn't like her. It left him no choice; he had to return.

He had phoned her from the airport, but with maddening impassiveness she said she'd tell him all about it when she saw him.

It was then he ran out of patience and slapped the receiver back on the hook. Then he glanced through the glass of the phone booth door and on through the waiting room window to the first swirls of snow, feeling a sudden agony of frustration and a fear that perhaps even when he saw her face to face she wouldn't tell him.

But of course she would tell him. In addition to her regular salary as his secretary, he paid her a bonus privately to keep him informed of things he might otherwise miss. He admitted he sometimes had to separate office gossip from office business, but that was only because she more than fulfilled her part of the bargain.

"What was that address again?" The taxi driver, who had been hunched over the wheel to peer through the fast-diminishing clear area of his side of the windshield, leaned back a little and cocked his head to one side for the answer.

"I didn't give any address," Devan said. "It's a tavern two blocks west of Inland Electronics, as I said. Know where that is?"

"Are you kidding? Inland takes up a whole city block."

"Then you should have no trouble finding it."

The driver gave him a look in the rearview mirror. It probably seemed strange to the driver that a man would get off a plane from Florida only to go to a cheap tavern just off Twenty-second Street. I could tell him I own the place, Devan thought. That would be more satisfying and believable than telling him the real reason.

But Devan said nothing. How could he explain why he should have given up the long, curved white beach at Pelican Rock? Only Beatrice Treat could say why and he would soon know the reason himself.

The cab double-parked in front of the Peacock tavern. Devan paid the driver and then held his hat firmly on his head as he lurched against the wind and went into the tavern.

He had never been there before and now that he looked around he wondered if he had been wise in suggesting it. Most of the confidential exchanges with Miss Treat had been within his own office, but at this hour—especially since he was presumably still basking in the Florida sun—it would not have been a very bright thing to do.

The Peacock was obviously so named because of the stuffed peacock in the window, a dusty and aging exercise in taxidermy, and replicas of it crudely painted on the walls. Several patrons at the bar glanced his way with indifferent eyes as he entered and then resumed their occupations. He looked to the dimly lighted booths at the rear as he stomped his feet lightly at the door. There was no mistaking Miss Treat and he saw her at once through the heavy shreds of smoke and walked toward her. Even as he did so, he saw the concern in her eyes.

"Mr. Traylor!" she said, rising. "Oh, I'm so sorry!" She looked more woebegone than he had ever seen her.

"Stop being sorry and sit down," Devan said gruffly, taking off his coat and hanging it beside hers on the booth hooks.

"But I can't help it!" She was on the verge of tears and when he sat down he put his hands comfortingly over hers. "I don't know whether I did the right thing or not, calling you, but I had to decide and I've thought about nothing else since and—"

A waitress came out of the haze and Devan ordered two bourbons, one with water and one with ginger ale.

"Please, none for me," Miss Treat said, raising the half-empty glass of ginger ale to explain. "It's—it's bad for my figure."

"You look as if you need it and you're going to drink it."

She looked white and drawn and as he patted her hand affectionately he was gratified to see a blush brighten her face. "Now why don't you tell me what all this is about?"

Miss Treat was a large woman, well over thirty, but she had not lost the grace and charm of a younger woman. It was this, plus her inexhaustible zest, efficiency and loyalty, that had made her an obvious choice for secretary when he first came to Inland. He had not been disappointed. He had often admitted that he could not have done as big a job as he had in three years without her. Simple and direct, she never faltered when it came to the good of Devan Traylor and Inland, though it had often meant embarrassment and loss of face to her.

He had never seen her in a veiled, pink-feathered calot before and he had to admit it complemented her black satin dress, which surprised him because she had always dressed so severely at the office.

"I don't know how to tell you," she said. "It's so involved. I knew I had to get you back before the board meeting. They're going to spend — up to a million dollars."

Devan winced. "A million dollars? For heaven's sake! What are they going to spend it for?"

"You left last week after the regular committee meeting. You remember."

Yes, he remembered. Routine business on the second Tuesday of the month. He'd signed papers and then shaken hands all around and left for his Oak Park residence to pick up Beverly and the kids to go to the airport. Everything seemed normal then.

"Well, they called a special meeting. But they couldn't get in touch with you because you'd gone. Not that they tried."

"Let me get this straight. You're speaking of the executive committee. Right?"

Miss Treat nodded. "Mr. Holcombe called the meeting at Mr. Orcutt's request. Mr. Basher, Mr. Holcombe, Mr. Tooksberry and Mr. Orcutt. That's all."

That would be the executive committee, except for Orcutt. Glenn Basher, youngish former Continental Electric man who'd been buying stock in Inland for years, James Holcombe, who had as divergent a record as Devan in electronics and administration and was also chairman of the board, and Howard Tooksberry, hardheaded counselor who had been with Inland since it got its state charter and who often stood in the way of advancement because things had a tendency to move too fast for him.

"What did they do?" Devan asked, bracing himself for the answer. Without him, Basher and Holcombe could have put anything over, even if Tooksberry dissented, which he did with monotonous regularity, for they would be the majority in Devan's absence. He had sided more than once with Tooksberry, forcing the committee to argue to wise decisions.

"They want to spend up to a million dollars, Mr. Traylor. A million dollars on a scientific experiment."

He could see form and substance now. There was Edmund G. Orcutt, president of Inland Electronics. He was a big, powerful man with a thick shock of white hair, beetling black brows and a thick mustache. Distinguished looking and impressive at the conference table. He had been hired because of an imposing record with a large radio-parts corporation, yet he had to be watched, Devan knew, because he had learned Orcutt was apt to be too liberal with company funds. He had talked with him about it on occasions. Now it appeared Orcutt had called a special meeting and had put through this thing that would now go to the board of directors as the recommendation of the executive committee, if he had understood Miss Treat correctly.

The board would rubber-stamp it, of course. It always did.

The drinks came and Devan emptied one shot glass into her ginger ale, stirred it absently with the muddler, pushed it to her.

"A million dollars. That's a lot of money. What kind of an experiment is it going to be, Miss Treat?"

"I don't know."

"You don't know? Weren't you there?"

Her face was pained. "That's the terrible thing about it, Mr. Traylor. They didn't even ask me to take the notes. All they did is ask me whether or not you had left town and I said you had and then they asked Miss Faversham to keep the notes."

"Who asked you if I had left town?"

"It was Mr. Orcutt."

"So that's the way it is." First, they make sure he's away and then they hold the meeting, making sure Miss Treat isn't there so she won't be able to report to him what went on. "If you weren't there, how did you find out what they talked about?"

"Well..."

"Never mind." He knew it would be a mistake to insist on knowing her sources. "Anyway, it gets more interesting every minute. What else did you find out?" He downed his drink, welcoming the warmth that went to work untying the worry knot in his stomach.

"The meeting was held on Monday. From what I could learn, the whole thing is secret. I don't know what else happened but I know they approved the expenditure."

She paused to sip her drink and he knew she was enjoying telling him these things. She'd tell it all in her own time. The bourbon was having a hard time with the knot. He wished she'd get on with what she knew, though he knew it would be useless to prod her.

"Oh, I forgot to mention Sam Otto. He was there."

So that was it! Devan hit his forehead with the flat of his hand. "Sam Otto! Now things are adding up. Why, that four-flushing, no-good gold-bricker. Don't tell me they fell for one of his schemes!"

"I don't know whether they did or not, but they're going to spend a million dollars and Mr. Otto was there."

"This is worse than I thought, Beatrice. Letting a con man like Sam put one over!" He lit a cigarette while the thought of Sam Otto made his muscles quiver in anger. He had put the quietus on a dozen Otto schemes. Small Sam Otto and his round, innocent face with its ever-present unlighted cigar. Sam Otto, the man who always makes five per cent when he makes a deal. Five per cent of a million is fifty thousand dollars! Sam had hit the jackpot.

"In fact, Mr. Traylor, Mr. Otto was there ahead of time."

"He would be. He never misses a chance."

"There was a Dr. Costigan with him. He's the scientist who is going to get the money."

"Don't speak so positively of it, Miss Treat. Nobody is going to get any money. We've got our own men and our own laboratory. Orcutt must be mad! I wonder if this Dr. Costigan exists."

"I just said he was there, Mr. Traylor."

"I know. But I'll bet he's some guy Sam picked up on skid row and paid a sawbuck for the walk-on part."

"He looked respectable."

Devan laughed. "You don't know Sam Otto. He's a front man from way back. A good one. I've got to give him credit. Either he waited until I was out of town or else he had Orcutt wait. Is that all you have to tell, Miss Treat?"

His secretary drank the last of her highball. He was glad to see her gray eyes were brighter and that there was color in her cheeks.

"Well, not exactly," she said. "Office talk is that Dr. Costigan is working in a building just south of the Loop. They say he claims our laboratories aren't big enough."

"Naturally. They can spend the money for the phony experiment with abandon out of sight of Inland." Costigan. For a moment the name clicked somewhere in his mind. Perhaps there was a Dr. Costigan after all, but he couldn't recall any in electronics. "What kind of an experiment do they think they're going to carry on?"

Miss Treat looked down at her empty glass. "I think it's just a joke, but I heard there was a lot of technical talk first and then they unfolded a drawing that looked like a space ship."

"A space ship! What does Inland Electronics want with a space ship?"

"That's what I keep asking myself, Mr. Traylor."

"Why the devil didn't you tell me this over the phone?"

"I wanted to, Mr. Traylor. Believe me, I did. But I just couldn't bring myself around to mention the space ship. It's so silly. And besides, I don't know that it's true."

"But you still could have mentioned about the million dollars."

"And then you'd have wanted to know what for and I'd have said space ships. I just couldn't, Mr. Traylor."

"All right." He ran a hand through his hair. It was going to take some doing to iron the whole thing out and separate the fact from the fiction.

"What are you going to do?"

"I don't know." The thing had gone only as far as the executive committee. He was thankful for that. They'd lose no time calling a board meeting, but he was there in time for that. He did not know just how far his written appeal to the decision of the executive committee would go even though he was a member of it. It would take a lawyer to figure that out. But *something* would have to be done. He'd have to make sure Sam Otto didn't get his money.

"Maybe," he said, "I'll explode a bomb in the office."

She looked at him so concernedly he was forced to smile.

"Not really. But I don't think we want to spend a million dollars on a space ship, do we?"

"I didn't think so."

"Besides, it would cost more than a million dollars to build a space ship. It looks like a phony deal all the way through, Miss Treat. I'm tackling Orcutt the first thing in the morning."

2

Devan had barely closed the heavy office door behind him when he saw the figure of Edmund Orcutt at
the end of the hall. Orcutt seldom missed a trick and
Devan knew that the man had probably already
learned he was in the building; now he was hurrying
toward Devan with those long strides of his, his face
friendly, his smile sincere and his eyes not in the least
surprised.

"Well, well, Devan!" Orcutt said warmly, moving
out from the corridor that led to the suite of executive
offices, his shoes noiseless on the thick carpeting of the
outer office.

"This *is* a surprise!"

Devan let him pump his hand as if he had been
gone a year. It was Orcutt's stock in trade, for he stead-
fastly held to the belief that you never know when the
hand you shake today may become the hand that helps
you tomorrow. Devan had grudgingly to admit it had
paid off more than once for Inland; there could be no
criticism of Orcutt's roster of influential friends.

"I thought you were in Florida and just the other
day I asked Miss Treat whether you had gone yet and

she said you had." Orcutt put his arm around Devan's shoulders as he talked and guided him to the corridor, turning to the secretary in the outer office momentarily.

"Mr. Traylor and I don't want to be disturbed, Miss Templeton."

When they were in the walnut-paneled office, Orcutt closed the door and said, "Whatever possessed you to come back, man? We're having terrible weather." He plopped into his leather chair and smiled amiably at Devan, rocking slightly.

"You know damn well why I've come back, Ed."

Orcutt sighed, rocked forward and started to fill a pipe. "I'm sorry you felt moved to come back, Dev. I thought you once told me you weren't indispensable. Don't you think we can get along without you for a while?" He studied Devan from beneath black brows as he lit his pipe.

"A million dollars, Ed, is a lot of money. And to Sam Otto, of all people!"

"You know about that, then. Some day I'll find out who feeds you information, as if I didn't have a good idea already." Orcutt smiled. "It was supposed to be a secret, but that's something you can't have around here. I should have known better. But really, Dev, you're wasting your time. There was no need to come back. You should be enjoying yourself in Florida. You worked hard enough for it."

"And let Inland lose a million dollars?"

It bothered Devan that Orcutt should continue to smile so confidently. The man seemed to be enjoying himself when he ought to be apologetic or at least explanatory.

"Inland isn't going to lose a cent, Dev."

"You bet it isn't. And do you know why? It isn't going to invest in research outside this building."

"Think so?"

"I know so." Devan had been standing. Now he sat in a leather-bottomed chair that hissed air when it received him. He drew another chair over and put his feet in it. "When is the board of directors' meeting?"

"This afternoon. You know something? It amazes me how you have found out so much, yet I know you haven't been near this place."

"This afternoon, eh? Aren't you pushing this thing a little?"

"I'm pushing it with all I've got, to be honest."

"Then what are you going to do when I go on record as opposing the recommendation of the executive committee?"

"That would certainly look silly, wouldn't it? It passed the committee, you know."

"Don't tell me Tooksberry voted for it."

"No. Can't say that he did."

"Well, then, the board will see that, since the committee passed it in my absence, it really is a draw. Two to two."

"But it won't count. You were notified of the meeting. It was all open and aboveboard. The fact that you were out of town was an unfortunate circumstance."

"You waited until I was out of town."

"Wait a minute, Dev!" Orcutt jerked the pipe out of his mouth and ashes cascaded from it. His eyes were cold and the corners of his mouth had frozen. "It's not like you to say things like that. Not like you at all. Besides, it's not true," Orcutt said grimly.

"Then will you please explain why it happened just after I went away?"

"I wish I knew how much you know about it so we could speak frankly. In case you don't know, it came up suddenly."

Devan laughed without humor. "I can see Sam Otto waiting until I leave town to rush up here and sell you a damn fool idea." He felt anger rising, got to his feet and went to the twin portholes, pushed the button that revolved the Polaroid screens so that he could look out into the assembly department.

Intricate little brains for guided missiles were being put together out there. Parts for computers and thinking machines, for devices as passé as radar alongside electronic gadgets that the public had not yet learned existed. But that was only one part of the plant. There were other places in the building where catalogued items for public sale were made. And there was one room where Inland put together a device that incorporated radioactive metal according to government specifications and not even Orcutt had any idea what it was for, whether it was complete in itself or became part of a larger mechanism. That was on the floor where most of the research was done.

He heard Orcutt clear his throat. "Maybe I can understand how you feel, Devan. I don't trust Sam Otto either. But you might as well know right now that it's not a damn fool idea."

Orcutt wasn't pleading. He talked as if he believed what he was saying. Whatever Sam Otto had done, Devan reasoned, he had certainly sold Edmund G. Orcutt.

"Look," Devan said, turning from the darkening windows. "I know Sam Otto better than you do. I've known him for years. He's been trying to sell me on gadgets and surprises and wonders ever since I first entered electronics professionally back in 1940. He even kept track of me when I was in the army to get me to back this idea or that when I got out. Not one of his contraptions was worth a damn. He doesn't care about that, though. He's just in it for what he can get out of it. He sticks you with a project, takes five per cent of the appropriation, skips out and leaves you with some screwball who never had anything in the first place while Sammy is out looking for another screwball who thinks he's got something."

"Sam Otto likes you," Orcutt said.

"To him I'll always be a potential sucker. He can't afford not to like me."

"He was disappointed you weren't at the meeting."

"I'll bet he was." Devan looked sharply at Orcutt. "Just how sold on this thing are you?"

Orcutt was wearing his smile again. "All the way, Dev."

Devan threw his hands in air. "I give up. I've always liked you, Ed. Now I don't understand you."

Orcutt opened a drawer, withdrew a few sheets of paper. "You mentioned five per cent. Take a look at this agreement. It hasn't been signed yet, of course, but it will be, after the board meeting this afternoon. I'll save you time by telling you you won't find Sam's name on it anywhere. Know why?"

"I'll bite."

Orcutt leaned across the desk. "He doesn't get a cent out of the appropriation."

Devan took the papers, riffled them, looked at a paragraph here and a paragraph there. A man named Dr. Winfield Costigan was to get a million dollars for an experiment he was to conduct. Devan threw them back on the desk.

"All right," he said. "What's Sam Otto in this thing for, then?"

"Sam believes in it, Dev. Same as I do."

Devan grunted. "I have to see that to believe it. Maybe this guy Costigan really sold *him* a bill of goods. Wouldn't that be a laugh after all these years! Selling Sam a space ship!"

"Space ship?" Orcutt stared at him for a moment, then broke into a hearty laugh that made tears come to his eyes. "That's rich, that is. The funniest thing I've heard in a long time. Your informant didn't get that one straight, Dev, but I can see how it happened. If you only knew, you'd be laughing, too."

"Well, what is it then?" Devan asked, reddening.

Orcutt's face sobered. "I can't tell you that, Dev. It's a matter of the utmost secrecy. All of us have agreed not to mention it here." Devan was getting more and more annoyed.

"Is that right? Want to know my opinion? I'd say Dr. Costigan and Sam Otto have you fellows all tied up with a pretty pink ribbon."

"You can think that if you want to, Devan, but right now I want you to take a trip with me."

"Where?"

"To Dr. Costigan's workshop."

Devan didn't move. "Ed, I value your opinion a lot, but nothing and I repeat *nothing* could be so earth-shaking that it can't be mentioned in the office of the company putting up the funds, much less in the presence of a member of the executive committee. Another thing: Why didn't you let Miss Treat take the notes for the meeting? Shall I tell you why? Because you knew she'd tell me all about it if you did."

"Now you're completely off the track, Devan. It was Miss Treat herself who turned down the note-taking task. She knew if she wasn't there it would sound more intriguing to you and make you hurry back."

"I don't believe it. Why should Miss Treat want me to hurry back?" Devan was exasperated. "You don't make sense, Ed."

"For heaven's sake, Dev! Can't you see it? The girl's in love with you! We've all seen it. We knew what was going on."

"Miss Treat?" Devan laughed. "Why, Ed, she can't be. I'm a married man. I have two children."

"Is that any criterion for love? Don't be so naive, Dev. She's been eating her heart out ever since you said you were going to Florida. She had a compulsion to get you back and she did."

"But she had a damn good reason, as far as I'm concerned, love or no love. She knew I wouldn't like the idea of Inland spending this money on a flight of fancy."

"Since we're being frank, Dev, let me tell you some-thing. You're just too damn sure of yourself. You're too certain you know everything. It so happens I'm staking my future in the field on this single venture." Orcutt knocked ashes from his pipe. "Now we might go and ask Jimmy about it, or we might mention it casually to Glenn and you'd see their reaction. But there's nothing like seeing the thing yourself. I knew you were coming and I've made the arrangements. So come on."

The building that Orcutt said the gadget was in was an old five-story brick factory that Devan guessed hadn't been used for at least three years. They circled the block several times in Orcutt's Cadillac, the big man swearing softly because all the parking spaces were filled.

"Some people park way down here and walk to their jobs in the Loop," Orcutt said, wheeling the car around another corner. "When we move in we're going to need space for company parking. But I don't see how we're going to get it."

Devan didn't say anything. Although he didn't want to prejudge the proposed project, he felt reasona-bly sure that his feeling about it would be justified. Whatever it was, there could be no reason to take it this far from Inland. There was plenty of room for research in the big plant and there'd be no parking problem there. Best of all, it would put the project underfoot, if there was to be a project.

They parked two blocks away and walked testily along hard-packed snow that covered the sidewalks. As they neared the empty building, they went past a tavern, a plumbing supply house with corroding copper tank floats and a disordered array of faucets, pipes and accessories behind dirty windows, a printing establishment with yellowed broadsides and type samples on display, a clean and white-painted front that proclaimed the building "Sudduth's Rescue Mission." There was a Bible in the window and a spotlight brightened the pages to which it was open. Next door was a grocery—Hodge's Grocery—dimly lighted, steamed-over plate glass spoiling the view inside.

Just below the ornate cornice topping the five stories of the next building, and spreading across the hundred-foot front were faded gold letters, "Rasmussen Stove Company," on a filigreed background. Some of the letters had, through years of weather, come loose and now were slanted, one against another. The "e" of "Stove" was missing. Devan wondered whatever had become of it.

"I don't think it's been a stove company for twenty years," Orcutt said, following Devan's look upward. "During the war, light tools were made here. Pliers and chisels. Come on." He approached the front door and knocked.

Devan saw that the old door was equipped with a new lock. Then he saw the door open a few inches. An old man with rheumy eyes, a face full of blue veins and wearing a muffler and earmuffs peered out at them.

"I'm Edmund Orcutt," Orcutt said. "Dr. Costigan is expecting us."

The door chain Devan hadn't noticed before was slid out and dropped. The old man stood in the doorway.

"Identification," he said.

"Identification?"

"Got to make sure," the man said, not moving aside. "Mr. Otto said to make sure."

"Sam Otto can go to hell," Orcutt said, drawing out his billfold and showing the old man who he was.

"How about him?" the old man said, pointing at Devan.

"He's with me."

The old man shook his head doubtfully. "I don't know about that. Mr. Otto—"

"Well, I do. We've got to come in. It's cold out here."

"It ain't any warmer inside." He stepped aside and when the two had stepped through he said, "Just a minute." Then he closed the door and rattled the chain in place. "I'd better go up with you."

The chill inside, as in any unheated building, seemed worse than the cold outside in spite of the fact that the old man had a portable kerosene heater working near his post at the door. Their breaths made large plumes of fog as they walked across the scarred floor to the rear of the dim interior. Here there were stairs that creaked and groaned as they walked up, the sounds jarringly loud because the building was empty.

In the middle of the second floor Devan saw a large, unpainted plywood shed with clean windows and fluorescent lights inside.

Several strands of braided electric wires ran from the structure's roof along the rafters and out a window that had lost its glass long ago. He could see no one inside the shed as they followed the door guard across the floor, but when they were nearly there the door was flung open and Devan saw Sam Otto.

It was the same Sam Otto, broad of face and broad of beam, his big teeth white in a wide grin, the cigar Devan knew would be there protruding from the ruddy face. The same eagerness, the same bright eyes. And, Devan guessed, the same glib tongue.

"Devan, Devan!" Sam came out as if to embrace him and, as Devan stepped to one side, caught an arm, found the hand and shook it. "Glad to see you. You, too, Mr. Orcutt. Dr. Costigan, we have visitors! Come in, come in. Plenty of room. Too cold out there." He dismissed the old man. "It's all right, Casey."

Sam bobbed on his feet impatiently and worried them into the room like a mother hen. "I know you, Devan. This one you'll never believe. But then Mr. Or-cutt didn't believe it either, did you, Mr. Orcutt?" He laughed and poked Orcutt in the ribs with his elbow. "I've really got something this time. Oh." He sensed the need of an introduction when Devan nodded to the fourth man in the room. "Dr. Costigan, this is Devan Traylor. Devan, I want you to meet Dr. Costigan. I'd better close that door. Got a heater in here, but it doesn't do too well when that door's open."

Devan shook the hand of a tall, slim man with thinning gray hair and moist gray eyes. The hand was limp, the body a little stooped, as if the doctor were embarrassed by his height. Devan guessed his age at around sixty.

"Pleased to meet you," Dr. Costigan said. His voice was low and soft. His manner was that of a shy man. "Are you with Inland, Mr. Traylor?"

"Is he with Inland?" Sam came up and slapped Devan on the back. "He's only one of the directors, Doctor, that's all. And a regular member of the executive committee, too."

The scientist looked at him with renewed interest.

"He was in Florida," Orcutt explained, shedding his coat. "Came back when he heard about the project."

"Oh, yes. The absent one." Dr. Costigan's smile was but a brief visitation. "They said there was one short."

"Didn't you tell Dr. Costigan we were coming?" Orcutt asked Sam with some annoyance.

"Never bother the doctor with unimportant details," Sam said. Then he laughed. "Not that Devan is an unimportant detail. Sure not. But the doctor has enough to think about. Think what he's got to do! I figured you'd get here when you got here. Now, a—"

"I just wanted the doctor to know what I had in mind," Orcutt said.

"Why, yes," Sam said. "Of course. The doctor knows, don't you, Doctor?" Dr. Costigan only raised his eyebrows, seemed about to say something when Sam went on. "How've you been, Devan?"

"I've been better," Devan said with a sickening feeling that he was wasting his time. The thing was getting more ridiculous all the time. He wished he had never come. "I suppose it's about time, isn't it, Sam, to show me that little outfit that turns blank paper into twenty dollar bills at the turn of a crank? Or is this the one that has an electric furnace that turns out real diamonds? Or a gold brick?"

"Always joking," Sam chuckled. "The same old Devan. You'll get a kick out of him, Doctor. Great joker."

Dr. Costigan looked alarmed. "Sam, I thought—"

Sam took out his cigar and put it on the edge of a desk. "How were we to know Mr. Traylor was coming, Doctor? Life's like that, isn't it? The unexpected and all that. A promise is a promise, I know, but then we must remember Mr. Traylor is an important man at Inland."

"But so many people!" The doctor was worried. "I told you I'd show it once and you agreed."

"But, Doctor! Mr. Orcutt's brought Devan all the way down here to see it."

"I don't blame you, Dr. Costigan," Devan said. "If I had my way, anything as important as the thing you have wouldn't be shown to anyone either. It wouldn't be so bad if I hadn't been through this many times before with Sam."

"Just a minute, Devan," Orcutt said. "I'm afraid I'm to blame, Dr. Costigan. I promised Devan he could see the machine." Then he went on firmly, "He's got to see it if we're going to get the approval of the board this afternoon." He looked at his wrist watch. "It's eleven now. The board meets at one thirty. There's a lot to be done."

Devan dropped into one of the chairs, lit a cigarette and looked at the three of them in disgust. "Look," he said. "I've been in the business for a good, long time. I doubt that anything merits all these shenanigans unless it is something better than the H-bomb. Whatever this thing is you have, cart it out and let's see it. I think you should know, Doctor, I think it's a phony deal all the way through and if you don't show this thing I'm going to tell the board just what I think of this whole setup."

"Devan," Sam said in a hurt voice. "You don't know what you're saying."

"Better let him see it, Doctor," Orcutt said. "Otherwise it looks like no deal."

For a moment Dr. Costigan stood in the middle of the room, his eyes bright with fury. Then he straightened and turned to a door on the far side of the room.

"Very well," he said, producing a key and inserting it into a large padlock.

Devan had an almost uncontrollable urge to laugh, but restrained himself. He looked at Orcutt and Sam and saw the eagerness in their faces and wondered how much of the act was for his benefit. When the doctor had the door open, Devan crushed out his cigarette and followed them through the door.

It was a small room, he guessed about ten feet by twelve, lighted by several fluorescent lights along the walls. There was a bench running along one side of it and tools familiar to the electronics trade were arranged neatly on the wall above.

The rear of the bench was littered with radio and electronics parts, items Devan recognized as a sweep generator, test instruments, oscilloscope, voltage control transformer, voltage stabilizer, and cabinets of resistor and capacitor assortments and other radio trivia. Except for the wall to the right with larger instruments in racks and a multitude of lights, buttons, switches and meters, it could have been an amateur's radio repair shop, although he would have been a well-heeled amateur.

In a corner of the room Dr. Costigan was bent over a large safe of the kind found in large factory offices. He had his back to the group, was furtively turning the combination. In a few moments he grabbed the handles and, with a grunt, swung the heavy door open.

Sam Otto moved to help, but the scientist waved him back. "I'll handle it."

Dr. Costigan reached in carefully, cradled a long metal device in his arms. It looked like a polished silver rocket about a foot in diameter, the circular base of the tube was broken by an arched opening that went all the way through.

The tall doctor struggled slowly across the floor with it and the others moved out of his way. He set it on the bench with a dull thud and then took hold of the tip and set it upright. At least it looks like a space-ship model, Devan said to himself with some amusement. Miss Treat had been right about that. It was about three feet high and the lights reflected brilliantly from its polished shaft.

The doctor busied himself with it, opening a bench drawer and taking out a number of patchcords, plugging them into jacks in the shaft and running the cords to a jack panel. As he worked, his long slim fingers expertly adjusted knobs and the slowness that Devan had taken for his usual manner was gone. Once, when the man turned to the meter panel, in the light from the glaring lights Devan could see a fanatic gleam in his eyes.

As the man worked, checking and rechecking, the breathing of all four of them seemed to become oppressively loud.

"Maybe I ought to open the door," Sam said. "It's getting a little stuffy in here."

"You will leave the door closed, please," Dr. Costigan said. "I'm nearly ready." Meter dials moved, needles fluctuated and somewhere inside the array of equipment, relays began to click. A motor started and ascended the scale in a faint hum.

"Now," the doctor said at last.

"Now what?" Devan asked sarcastically.

"You just wait," Sam said.

"For heaven's sake, Devan," Orcutt said. "Give the doctor a chance."

"Now, Mr. Traylor," Dr. Costigan said. "If you will, please."

Devan moved to the bench and Orcutt and Sam made room for him.

"You see that hole at the bottom," Dr. Costigan was pointing to the archway at the bottom of the bullet-shaped shaft. "Look through it. I'll wiggle my fingers on the other side. So."

Devan bent down. "I'll be damned!" he said.

"What did you see?" Sam asked, surprised.

"I can see his fingers on the other side."

"Sam is right. You are a funny man, Mr. Traylor. Now." The doctor cleared his throat. "Put your finger in the hole."

Orcutt and Sam pressed close to watch, but Devan did not do as the doctor said.

"First, you tell me what's going to happen."

The doctor shook his head. "No. You will not be hurt. Go ahead. Go ahead." He pushed Devan's hand to the hole.

Again Devan hesitated, looked around at them. They were expectant, waiting. He shrugged, shoved his finger in the hole. He felt nothing, withdrew it.

"Is everybody happy?" he asked.

"You didn't look at your finger while you did it," the doctor protested.

"Come on, Devan," Orcutt said impatiently. "Don't grandstand now."

Devan put his finger near the hole again. There was room enough for his whole hand but he put only his finger in and watched.

The finger vanished.

Astonished, he quickly withdrew his finger and looked at it. It was still whole. His heart quickened. He put his finger in again, saw it disappear. Then he thought his finger felt cold, withdrew it and felt of it with his other hand.

His finger *was* cold.

This is a trick, Devan thought. In a moment they'll be giving me the big horse laugh. He turned to look at each face. Dr. Costigan's eyes mocked his. Sam Otto had a benign grin. Orcutt was excited, his eyes bright.

Devan bent down and looked through the hole. He could see nothing but smooth sides of metal, ran his finger around the edge of the hole. It was finely machined, very smooth.

He doubled his fist, backed away a little and moved his fist close to the hole, then into it. He kept going until his arm was in the hole up to his shoulder. He brought his other hand around to meet the hand on the other side.

His hand wasn't there. Only his empty sleeve.

Frantically, he bent his arm in the hole. It met nothing but air where the sides of the archway opening should have been. Then he felt the cold. It was as if he had put his arm through a hole in a window to the outside.

He withdrew his arm in a hurry.

It was very cold.

3

Devan stared at the pointed cylinder of silver and as he did so his vision blurred and the shaft shimmered in the light. His mind, confronted with what his senses had recorded there, rejected it as impossible, yet he could not disqualify his eyes and his hand. He had to believe either his mind or what he had physically experienced. He was conscious of sweat collecting on his skin, of the rapid beating of his heart, the feel of nerves drawn tight.

He did not *want* to believe what he had just seen, what he had just done, but there seemed no alternative. But if he believed, then he had no basis for objecting to the project. If it was a trick, and he felt certain such a trick would ultimately be revealed, then he could never forgive himself for being such a fool for believing. But how to disprove it? How to show that it was a fraud?

His mind whipped back to the time he had seen a magician working seeming miracles on a stage. The man sawed a woman in half, caused an elephant to disappear, floated a woman upward over the audience, firing a gun at her when she neared the top of the theater, the woman vanishing, the clothes she had been wearing floating slowly and softly to the heads of the amazed spectators below.

Impossible? He had seen a magician do it. But he had not done it himself. There was a difference there. A few minutes ago he had inserted his arm into a hole through a polished metal cylinder and only his empty coat sleeve came out the other side.

"Well...?" Sam's voice had an upsweep.

Damn you, Devan thought. You're really pushing me, aren't you! You want me to commit myself right away, don't you? He turned slowly, angry because they were working against him, had deliberately led him on and he had taken the bait. Well, they wouldn't catch him that easily.

"Dr. Costigan," he said. "Will you please turn your gadget ninety degrees on the bench? Can you do that without pulling out any of those patchcords?"

The doctor rubbed his chin, looked at him speculatively. "I guess so." He moved the cylinder closer to the panels, turned it as Devan had directed.

"And do you have a trouble light, Doctor?"

"Trouble light?"

"Work light. Something I can see into the hole with. One with a cord long enough to reach here."

The doctor rummaged through a drawer, brought out a caged light on the end of a cord. Devan plugged it into a nearby socket, turned on the light.

"Now, Ed, if you don't mind, would you please reach into that thing while I view the operation from this side?"

He bent over so his ear was on the bench, adjusted the light before him so that the opening was blazing with light and he could see through it clearly.

Orcutt moved to the other side of the cylinder.

"Now," Devan said. He watched as Orcutt's extended fingers moved in the light toward the hole, saw an incredible thing happen when the fingers passed the opening archway. The fingertips disappeared and the bones, blood vessels and muscles were clearly visible as if cut off at the opening. As the fingers advanced, the cross section moved past the knuckles to the palm, then the wrist.

As the arm went in, the coat sleeve around it became limp, dropped to the surface of the bench and slid along in the hole as Orcutt pushed farther in. Finally, the sleeve came out Devan's side and moved toward him a few inches and stopped when Orcutt could put his arm in no farther.

Devan reached over, pulled hard on the sleeve.

"Hey!" Orcutt yelled, drawing back.

"No, don't draw your hand out."

"But it's getting cold in there."

"Well, hold it a minute longer."

Devan dropped the sleeve, turned out the light, set it on the bench, then inserted his own hand into the opening. He had difficulty in forcing his hand in until he pulled Orcutt's empty sleeve out; otherwise the bunched sleeves prevented further entry. With his other hand he held Orcutt's sleeve taut and pushed his hand into the chamber, finding Orcutt's arm. It was bare and cold. Orcutt had bent his elbow and now

Devan did, too, and they clasped hands as in Indian wrestling.

Satisfied, Devan dropped his hand, felt along Orcutt's arm, first the wrist, then the forearm, pulling the hair there. Orcutt winced.

"What's the idea, Dev?"

"Just testing," Devan said, smiling in spite of himself.

He moved his hand along the arm to the elbow, up the elbow to... the flesh ended, cut smooth as if by a microtome at the other opening. He ran his fingers over the stub of the arm. The surface was like glass and just as unyielding.

"Feel that?" Devan asked.

"Vaguely."

"All right," Devan said, withdrawing his arm.

Orcutt took his arm out, started to massage it.

"Damn! It's cold in there."

"Are you convinced, Mr. Traylor?" It was Dr. Costigan.

Devan nodded. There was no denying it now.

"Well, Devan?" It was Sam again.

Devan watched while the doctor disconnected the many patchcords, unable to phrase an answer. His thoughts were too chaotic, the experience too recent to make sense saying anything. It was like watching a fascinating play or reading an engrossing book and when it was over wishing it could have gone on because reality was so much less interesting, yet knowing there had to be an end and, once it had come, trying to bring the lesser things of one's environment into focus and proper perspective again.

"I guess it has made an impression on Devan," Orcutt said. "I know it's hard to believe, Dev, but it's true. You came prepared for something much less. Now you've seen the improbable and it's got you going."

Devan sighed. "You're right. It's impossible. Only it isn't. I've seen it." He fingered a cigarette out of his pack, lit it absently. "How many others have seen it, Ed?"

"The rest of the committee."

"And Tooksberry voted against it?"

Orcutt nodded. "He doesn't believe it. He wouldn't go near it. Glenn and Jimmy were sold right away."

The doctor had the silver shaft in his arms again, carried it to the safe. Devan could not keep his eyes off the thing, was glad when at last the safe door swung shut and the doctor was turning the knob.

"Let's go to the other room," Sam said, opening the door. A blast of cooler, more breathable air swept into the room and it cleared Devan's head.

When they were seated in chairs in the outer room, Devan wiped his perspiring forehead with his handkerchief.

"I really think the thing's got you, Dev," Orcutt said, laughing.

"You look as if you need a drink."

"How did you feel when you saw it?"

"Much the same way." Orcutt glanced at his wrist watch. "It's nearly noon. The board meeting's at one thirty. We've got to get moving."

"We could eat up here," Sam said. "I could put in a call for something."

"Did I hear someone mention a drink?" Dr. Costigan was sitting up straight in his chair.

Devan looked around, saw no bottles or glasses. "I could stand one. Do you have to send out for it?"

"Just a moment." The doctor went to the padlocked door again. When he returned with a bottle of whiskey, they asked him where he got it. "In the safe," he explained.

"He keeps it right next to the silver tube," Sam said as the doctor arranged four small glasses on the desk. "I don't know which he considers more valuable."

"Mr. Otto has known me but briefly, gentlemen," Dr. Costigan said, almost gay. "There are facets to my character that are quite interesting."

Devan was gratified to see that Dr. Costigan was loosening up. Perhaps he was a man who did not care for new people, a man who had to get a bit used to you first.

"Here's to Dr. Costigan's tube," Sam Otto said, lifting the half-filled glass.

As they drank, Devan noticed the ease with which Dr. Costigan downed his whiskey.

"How does the tube work, Doctor?" Devan asked. "I've seen just about everything in electronics, but this is a new one on me."

The doctor smiled craftily. "That would be telling, wouldn't it?"

"Dr. Costigan's very quiet about what makes the wheels go around, Devan," Sam said, retrieving his cigar from the desk edge and chewing the end of it. "He'd been trying to get funds from several big companies when I caught up with him. He wouldn't even tell them what it was supposed to do."

"I'll be frank," the doctor said. "I've got no head for business. I knew I'd run into trouble."

"I dropped in on Joe Gordon at National a couple weeks ago," Sam went on. "I took him out to dinner and while we were eating he mentioned the doctor's name. He said he was one of the screwiest guys he'd ever seen—you'll pardon me, Doctor, but that's just what he said—because Joe said the doctor wanted the dough without even putting on a show, just saying he had something new. Can you beat that?"

Devan grunted. "Knowing you, Sam, you couldn't let a thing like that go by. You hotfooted it right over to see the doctor."

"Of course!" Sam beamed, the cigar held tightly in the big teeth. "If I hadn't, where would we be now? Sure, I hurried over to his place. Basement of his house on the North Side. Had the thing right out in the open on the workbench. Can you imagine that?"

"Best place in the world for it," the doctor argued. "Nobody'd expect anything like that there."

"Well, you were still taking a chance. Anyway, I argued him into letting me see it. Then I had to work on him to show me what it did. I about fell over when I stuck my finger in."

"For once you had something," Devan said. "Do I understand right? Are we buying it for a million dollars?"

"No," Orcutt said. "That comes later. We're only advancing the money for the experiment."

"The experiment? Here we go again. Why do we have to experiment?"

Orcutt laughed. "Exactly what I wanted to know, Dev. Sam said the doctor wanted around a million dollars to experiment with and—of course I'd seen the demonstration already—and I said the gadget was complete as it is. Besides, I couldn't see spending a million dollars when the thing was already finished. I couldn't see any immediate application for it. But the doctor had other ideas. Why don't you tell him, Doctor?"

Dr. Costigan cleared his throat, leaned back in his chair until it touched the wall, looking, Devan decided, like a farmer passing the time of day at the country grocery store.

"What's the tube good for?" The doctor shrugged. "I asked myself that a thousand times and at first received no reasonable reply. So I started to work out some things. The best idea is that it can be used to diagnose internal diseases, cancers and the like. You run a body through it and you get a cross section of the insides and you can examine every part without the expense, danger or mess of an exploratory operation. There are ways it could be set up so that a microscope could examine the cross sections, but the vanishing region would have to be concentrated in a thin, fan-shaped beam. You understand that only living tissue goes through, don't you, Mr. Traylor? No dead things. No minerals or metals."

"That accounts for the coat sleeve, then," Devan said. "But what about the outer layer of skin and the fingernails and the hair I felt on Orcutt's arm? That's all dead tissue."

Dr. Costigan's smile, which exposed yellowed teeth and a few gold crowns, lasted longer than usual.

"I'll answer that in a moment. To get on with this other thing about doctors using it to explore human anatomy, at once a great question arises. What happens to the part of the body that disappears?" The doctor's eyebrows went up like window shades. Then they came down again and he leaned forward.

"You've only seen what went on *here,*" he said in a confidential tone. "Let me tell you what happened when I first discovered this thing. My wife and I were living in a different house and I was experimenting with an even smaller outfit in the basement. I put my finger in the hole and it disappeared, just as it does here. The difference is that I felt something wet, though my finger always came out dry.

"Curious, I made the hole bigger by making a bigger tube. Took me more than a year to make the outfit you've seen. When I first put my whole arm in this one and moved my arm around, I could feel water. It swirled around. Yet, when I took my arm out, it was dry. Can you figure out what my next step should have been?"

The doctor looked at them expectantly, as if he were waiting for someone to speak up like a bright student with the answer. Nobody wanted to guess it.

"I took a white mouse. I held it tight, put it in the hole, felt the mouse struggle. Then it was still. I tried to get my hand out with the mouse in it, but my hand would not cross the barrier with it. The mouse had drowned and dead things, I discovered, would not come through. I had to let it go in order to get my hand out."

Devan lit a cigarette, glanced at Orcutt. Orcutt smiled.

"We moved to a house on the North Side. I started experimenting again. There my hand met air, not water. I got another mouse, moved it through the hole and back again. No ill effects. Then I tied the mouse down on its back on a board, moved it halfway into the hole, took it out. The mouse had come free at the end that went into the hole. The knots were still there but the mouse's feet were not in them.

"I had a better idea. I tied the mouse down again, let the end that came free thrash around in the hole, injected nembutal into an artery on this side of the hole. The mouse died. I tried pulling it out, but it wouldn't move. I nearly pulled its body apart trying to get it out; the invisible dead part in the hole wouldn't cross the barrier. I could push the visible dead half into the hole clear over to the other opening and it remained visible. Only when I turned the machine off did it come free — the dead half on this side. It was cut as if by a razor. So, you see? There are definite scientific laws regulating this thing. I am only beginning to discover what they are. As long as the dead tissue is attached to living tissue and is a part of it, it will pass; if the whole organism is dead, it will go neither way." Dr. Costigan paused.

"The point the doctor wants to make, Dev," Orcutt said, "is that this would be a standard piece of equipment in hospitals but who would want to use it if he didn't know where the disappearing part of his body is going?"

"It could be Afghanistan or the Black Sea," Sam said.

"It doesn't make any difference where," Orcutt said. "But people will want to know *just* where."

"I've thought about it a lot," Dr. Costigan said, pouring himself a little more whiskey. "Does the tube merely render living things invisible? Does the tube go back in time? Does it go to the future? To a coexistent plane? To some other planet? To some other place on this one? Suppose you stuck your hand in the hole and it came out in the vacuum of outer space?"

One fluorescent light, which blinked once in a while, made a tinkling click as it did so, the only sound in the room for a few moments as they sat there, each obviously considering where the place might be.

"The experiment, then," Devan said. "That will be to determine where the body goes?"

"It would be so simple if we could just send a TV set through the hole," Orcutt said. "Or a periscope."

"Has anybody any idea of how we are going to find out where the living tissue goes?" Devan asked.

"We've got to build a large enough tube to let a man go through, Dev," Orcutt said. "His whole body."

"He can report back what he sees," Dr. Costigan said.

"That's what the million dollars is for."

"Who knows where that hole goes to, what fabulous things might be seen once a man goes through? Perhaps he'll meet people from the future, people from the past."

The doctor's eyes looked far away. "It's beyond imagining what that man will find, gentlemen."

"It's going to be difficult presenting this thing without telling the board the whole story," Orcutt said, his hand hovering over the choice of three pipes in the rack on his desk. "But I think you'll all agree it shouldn't be done."

"Definitely not," Sam said. "I was a newspaperman once and I know what those fellows would do if they found out about it."

The telephone rang and Glenn Basher picked it up. "Thanks, Miss Treat," he said, dropping it back into its cradle on a corner of Orcutt's large desk. "O'Grady's here. We can check him off." He put a mark by the name on the sheet of paper before him. "Four more and they'll all be here."

"We don't have to worry about the board, Ed," Devan said. "I don't see how they could go back on our recommendation."

Howard Tooksberry, whose chair was a little distant from the others, snorted. "It's not right," he said, adjusting his glasses on the bridge of his nose. "The board should be apprised of the whole thing."

"But you can't—you mustn't do that!" Sam said excitedly. "Why...!"

"You're wrong there, Howard," James Holcombe looked up from the diagram of the enlarged tube, fixing the man with steady, blue eyes. "Do you realize what it would mean if the public caught wind of this thing? Sam Otto's right. The reporters would be knocking down the doors. No, if you tell the board, there's bound to be a leak somewhere. As far as I know, no other concern is even thinking about a thing like this. Let's not get them started."

"It's pretty well set, then, gentlemen?" Orcutt swung his head to survey their faces one at a time. Tooksberry would not look at him. "We're to state it is an experiment in force field effects on living tissue which may result in new medical practices, that Dr. Costigan here has been charged by the executive committee to handle the project. He'll produce, on the basis of what our experts have said, an entirely new approach to internal medicine. That ought to do it."

"It's gobbledegook," Devan said. "Unless you know just what the words mean. Then it makes sense."

"I don't know how else you can tell them," Sam said. "The doctor and I were faced with the same thing trying to explain it to Mr. Orcutt. We couldn't say too much, we couldn't say too little."

"*Ultra vires*," Tooksberry said.

Everybody looked at him.

"Just what the hell do you mean by that, Howard?" Orcutt said.

"Just what I said." Tooksberry looked them over coldly. "*Ultra vires* means to exceed your vested authority as officers and board members under the corporate charter. It seems to me that's just what you're doing. You could be sued for it."

"Look," Orcutt said, leaning across the desk. "You saw the gadget. Don't you believe in it?"

"What have you got against the doctor and me?" Sam asked. "You've been against us from the first."

"Howard enjoys being contrary," Basher chided. "He revels in it. If we had an outfit for making gold out of lead he'd vote against it."

"All right," Tooksberry said, rising, his face angry. "You asked for it, now I'll tell you what I think. First of all, why does Dr. Costigan want to experiment? Second, why doesn't he reveal to us what makes the thing work, if it does work? Third, suppose it does prove to be of value? What's to prevent Dr. Costigan from taking the fruits of Inland's million dollars and setting himself up in business? Where do we come in on the profits? The trouble with all of you is that you're too curious about the experiment and not curious enough about where the money comes in."

Howard Tooksberry sat down heavily, took off his glasses and started to polish them nervously.

Sam Otto, whose face had become whiter with every word, now stood up, fists clenched, teeth together on his cigar. He advanced a step toward Tooksberry.

"Sit down, Sam!" Orcutt said firmly. He lit his pipe as Sam took his seat, blew out the match with smoke. "I think your points are pretty well taken, Howard. As you usually do, you insert some practical ideas into what might otherwise be entirely too theoretical and enthusiastic a discussion.

"The trouble is that, since you've been against the project, you haven't been in on some of the informal discussions on the matter. So I'll bring you up to date. You ought to know this, too, Devan.

"Sam Otto and Dr. Costigan came to me last Friday and explained something about what they had. They insisted I see the thing. Otherwise they were going to give it to Westinghouse or General Electric or one of the other big companies. I've seen too many corporations fold by passing up something that eventually spelled success in capital letters for their competitors.

"You were out of town, Devan, so, although we had all made plans to do other things, Glenn, Jimmy, Howard and myself all went to see the thing firsthand. Everybody was impressed but Howard. We agreed to hold an executive committee meeting the first thing Monday morning, which we did, going through the motions so that it would be a matter of record, scheduling the full board for this afternoon.

"In the meantime, Glenn and Jimmy and myself have been talking to Sam and Dr. Costigan informally. If the thing is perfected for medical use and for all subsequent uses that may develop as a result of what we find out from the experiments, Dr. Costigan is to get fifteen per cent of the net profits, Sam Otto ten per cent and the remainder goes to Inland.

"Dr. Costigan may reveal the secret of his tube if he wants to, but he has asked to be the proprietor of it exclusively, and to this we have agreed. A sealed copy of the detailed plans for his tube is to be put in the Inland vault, however, in the event of his death so that Inland will not lose what has been started. We will take over the experiment ourselves in that event. Dr. Costigan has agreed not to enter the manufacturing field for twenty-five years following the signing of the agreement this afternoon. Does that answer some of your questions, Howard?"

"Yes." Tooksberry had said the word he had to say and the necessity for it made him sullen. "It's true I didn't know all about that. But for the record, I still vote against it."

Sam was distressed, pounded a fist into a palm absently. Dr. Costigan could only look at the man in surprise.

Tooksberry's eyes challenged them all. "I still say it isn't fair to let Dr. Costigan conduct the experiments the way he wants to. There are a lot of engineers here in the plant who could render valuable assistance. Besides, I just don't like the way the whole thing is being handled."

The ring of the telephone interrupted again. Glenn Basher checked off two more names.

"I don't mean to be personal, Doctor," Devan said. "But there is something I've been wanting to ask you."

"What is it?"

"How did you come to invent this tube? Are you a Ph.D.? Is research just a side line?"

"You mean you don't know about the doctor?" Sam asked in amazement. "Why, Dr. Costigan is well known. He—"

"Let the doctor talk, Sam."

Dr. Costigan smiled. "Sam is the most loyal man I ever met, Mr. Traylor. But sometimes he gets a little excited about things. No offense, Sam. As for the tube, I'll tell you the story of it some day. It may interest you. For the Ph.D., I got it at Claybourne Technical College in 1922. It was in physics. I taught at Dewhurst until two years ago when our children were grown and married and there seemed no necessity for teaching any longer. So my wife and I left Dewhurst, moved back to Chicago here where my wife's sister is an invalid, moved in with her. We bought a better home on the North Side recently, but it left me with only a little income and I wanted to continue working with the tube. There was nothing else to do but ask financial assistance and that is where Sam came in."

Sam nodded. "Something you don't know, Devan: I've sunk everything I have in it. I've leased the building for a year, built the office on the second floor, bought the safe and hired old Casey."

The phone jangled and before it had given a full ring Basher had it in his hand. A moment later he put it down.

"Everybody's in the conference room," he said. "We'd better get up there."

"Quarter to two," Orcutt said, glancing at his wrist watch. "I'll bet we'll have it signed, sealed and delivered in half an hour." He glanced at Tooksberry. "Unless somebody interferes."

"I'm not changing my vote," Tooksberry said. "But I still don't like it. But I won't reveal any of your precious secrets, if that's what's worrying you."

4

Edmund Orcutt was wrong. Instead of passing the board of directors of Inland Electronics in half an hour, the matter of funds for the Costigan project was approved in twenty-eight minutes. A great deal of the success of the proposal's acceptance lay in Orcutt's presentation. He explained that the money was to be used for research in force fields. He spoke glowingly of the unknown possibilities that existed therein, particularly of the probable financial gains for Inland, but he carefully let each member imagine for himself just what form the physical possibilities assumed.

Devan watched the board members as Orcutt talked. Spencer O'Grady, a wizened old man with purple veins in his forehead, was doodling on a paper before him, as he always did. Mrs. Charles Petrie, who never came to a board meeting without her knitting, was busy with her yarn, another good sign, the needles clicking in monotonous rhythm. She never looked up. Homer Parrett, his hands behind his head and his chair tilted away from the table, unconcernedly smoked his cigar and looked at the wall with a vacant stare while Clarence Gleckman chewed his gum savagely and stared at Orcutt. Nothing unusual there. Other members were occupied in other customary attitudes. Devan decided there was no need to worry.

When Orcutt had finished and Chairman Holcombe asked for a discussion, Mrs. Petrie put her knitting down and looked up the long table.

"You said the executive committee voted for it, didn't you, Mr. Holcombe?"

"Yes, ma'am."

"Well, that's enough for me. I don't understand what it's all about. But then I seldom do."

"A million dollars is a lot of money," Mr. Parrett said, never taking his eyes off the opposite wall, never taking the half-smoked cigar out of his mouth or letting all four of the chair legs touch the floor at the same time.

"You have to spend money to make money," Mr. Gleckman countered in a gravel voice. "We've done it before."

Two minutes later the largest amount of money ever to be appropriated by Inland in Devan's experience was a matter of record and the board members moved out of the conference room one by one and out the opened doors with them moved the long shreds of cigar and cigarette smoke that had collected beneath the lights.

The board had been so amenable to suggestion that Devan could now see how a handful of men could wreck a corporation, something that had never occurred to him before. Yet Inland board members had every reason to believe in the executive committee; it had not failed them yet. That is why the shareholders elected the same people year after year—that and the large dividend checks. But Devan wondered how the board would have acted if Orcutt had tried to explain *exactly* what the money was to be used for. You can't tell people you want to send a man through a hole in a million dollar tube and expect them to understand what you're talking about.

There were drinks for the executive committee in Orcutt's office and even sour-faced Howard Tooksberry took one and relaxed a little. Devan excused himself after two drinks and Dr. Costigan, who was on his fourth, shook his hand warmly as he left. He managed to escape Sam Otto, who was trying to outdo the scientist and was beginning to slobber a little.

In his own office, Devan told Miss Treat to go home and pack for her first space ship ride. Then he took a bottle of bourbon from his desk drawer and prepared a drink, which he consumed in solitary satisfaction.

He could go back to Florida and be with Beverly and the kids. And he knew he should go back. But somehow the idea of the tube and what it was going to do appealed to him more. There was the thrill of something new there, some province as yet completely unexplored by man, discovered by a relatively obscure physics teacher named Dr. Winfield Costigan.

Industrial news, as does other news, especially the kind that one tries to keep private, travels fast. There is an unseen network of nerves running from one manufacturing plant to another over which research results, project proposals and policy decisions are communicated. Nobody knows how but everybody knows why.

Perhaps it is because of the Miss Treats of the world, the people who are paid to report what they see and hear, that such communication is possible.

Now that the decision had been made and the money appropriated, there was no reason for delay, Devan reasoned. He could help see to it that sure-to-be obstacles were overcome. Inland would have to buy the Rasmussen Stove Company building, for example. And some system would have to be devised to keep the project continually under wraps. People would have to be hired. The right kind of people. The problems that came to his mind were endless.

He picked up the phone and dialed for long distance. In a few minutes he was talking to his wife.

"What was it all about, Dev?" she asked. "Was it as bad as Miss Treat hinted? I've been waiting, wondering what happened."

"The crisis is over," he said. "Everything's all right. Everything's all ironed out."

"When are you coming down, then?"

He coughed. "Well, not right away. I—"

"Then everything's *not* all right."

"Look, Beverly, we have a new project. It's a big thing. Nothing like it before. I want to see that it gets going right. It shouldn't mean more than a few days, not more than a week. I'll fly down."

"Oh, Dev!" The voice broke a little. "I've been lonely since you've been gone. I don't really know anybody in this town. I'm nothing without you!"

Devan could envision her blue eyes welling up with hot tears. The thought moved him.

"You've got the kids."

"But they miss you, too."

"I miss them," he said gruffly. "It's not as if I'm going to be gone all winter. I'm going to be needed here."

"Are you sure you're not needed here more, Dev?"

"Would you like to come back with the children?" He was half angry.

"You know that wouldn't be right, interrupting their school again."

"No, I suppose it wouldn't. Look, Beverly, just a few days. I'll be down."

He could hear her crying and, while it touched him and made him miserable for what he felt he had to do, he resented the coercive factor that he considered tears to be.

"Beverly... are you still there?"

"Yes," she sobbed. "And you're still there."

"Stop behaving like a child and listen to me," he scolded. "I'll rush through these preliminary things and fly down as soon as possible. A week at the most. Do you hear?"

"All right. Please make it soon."

Devan stood across the street from the Rasmussen Stove Company building and decided that the work he had helped plan two months before had gone well.

To the casual eye the building probably looked much as it had for the past twenty years, but he knew a studied examination would reveal certain changes. Old glass had been replaced all around with frosted glass, for one thing, along with other exterior improvements he had suggested.

He knew that neighborhood people must have been witness to a subtler, more extensive change that did not show from the outside. If his plans had been carried out during the past sixty days, there should have been feverish activity inside, ready-mixed concrete trucks should have rolled up to the rear entrance at regular intervals around the clock, shifts should have reported for work three times a day and smoke should have flowed from the chimney in an endless ribbon across the sky.

To Loop-bound workers and area residents the building still stood, though it was now obviously occupied. How was anyone to guess two buildings stood now where one had stood before? And if they did guess it, could they also guess why?

Like a nesting block, a strong, reinforced concrete building was completed inside. That much he could be sure of. The outside brick was merely the outer shell, the camouflage for the inner building twenty feet smaller on all sides. But the old floors between it and the outer walls had been retained; otherwise the shell might have collapsed. As it was, the floors made a corridor running around its perimeter on each level.

There were a lot of things he knew ought to be finished by now, but he had had no way of knowing how they had come along. Orcutt's letters had been too general, his telephone conversations too guarded to tell much. He had been aching to get back, had been anxious to know.

He pulled his hat down to withstand the stiff, late March breeze, crossed the street and entered the building.

"Mr. Traylor!" A girl whose name he could not remember was at the information desk and she rose and smiled at him. He saw that the concrete wall was hidden by paneling, as he had suggested, and that the area between it and the front of the building was occupied with a random array of desks. "You *are* Mr. Traylor, aren't you?"

"Yes." He returned her smile and stepped through the gate. "How is everything?"

"Just fine." The girl moved back a bit when he came through. She was ill at ease. He was a crisis. "I have to be sure about the identity, Mr. Traylor."

"Yes, of course." He fished in his billfold for his driver's license. "I've forgotten your name."

"I'm Dorothy Janssen." She took his license in trembling fingers.

"You used to be at the West Side plant, didn't you?"

"Yes." She returned the card, seemed much relieved and when she smiled this time she gave him the five dollar one. "Thank you, Mr. Traylor."

"You keep on being sure of people, do you hear?"

No one bothered him when he went through the door on the right that he knew opened to a corridor that ran the length of the building. On the right was the wall of the old building, on the left the rough concrete of the inner building.

At the rear were the same stairs he and Orcutt had climbed to get to the plywood shed on the second floor, but he knew the shed was no longer there. A much bigger room replaced it.

Devan turned left and crossed the old wood floor to a small doorway in the inner wall. It was next to a closed entranceway that was big enough to admit the largest truck made.

He pushed the red button in the wall. A moment later the door started to open and he walked into a small, softly lighted room, the door hissing to a loud click shut behind him. A clean-cut, neatly uniformed man in a recessed office space came to the waist-high counter.

"Miss Janssen in the front office said you'd be back here, sir," he said. "I have a badge for you. Will you sign in, please?"

Devan wondered where they had dug up the old picture of him as he pinned the identification to his lapel. Then he signed his name in the book, putting the time in the proper column. He noticed there was also a column for entering the time one left the inner building.

The plant policeman pressed a buzzer and Devan walked past the opening door.

The big room took his breath away, though he knew exactly what it was going to look like. He had to stop and look at it; seeing it and planning it, he decided, were two different things.

The walls of the room rose nearly five stories and seemed taller than the outside building simply because nothing broke the smoothness of the reinforced concrete. There were at least a hundred lights blazing in

the ceiling, erasing shadows of objects and men working on the ground floor. The room reminded him of the
Pennsylvania Station and a mixture of recollections of
other large places, yet he knew it could not possibly
compare with any one of them.

The sounds in the room were deafening—the nerve-
shattering howl of drills, the clatter of riveters, the
banging of hammers and other construction noises he
could not identify and not all of which he could see.
The men who had constructed the building had done
their work fast and well and were, he was glad to see,
completely out of the way. In the center of the vast
room, scaffolding was going up and already a few
pieces of the bottom of the giant Costigan tube were
being put in place.

Behind him was the electrically operated steel-
doored entranceway and the small office through
which he had just passed. Along the wall on his right,
workmen were installing control panels. On his left
were the project offices, concrete boxes built out from
the wall. A vast project, no matter how you looked at
it. All a man had to do was poke his nose in here and
he'd see how big it was.

He moved now to one of the offices along the left
wall, the last and largest in the line. That would be Dr.
Costigan's. As he walked across the floor, he was surprised to see many strange faces. He nodded or waved
to those he knew.

When he closed the door of the scientist's sound-
proof office and stood just inside, he saw that the
physicist was not there, which surprised him because

he thought Dr. Costigan would live with the job until it was done.

A young woman who had been bent over a drafting table, running a line out with a ruling pen, turned to him.

"Dr. Costigan isn't here," she said, brushing a lock of hair from in front of an eye. "Is there anything I can do?"

Devan had never seen her before, found himself interested in the way her dark blue eyes looked into his, the graceful way she had pushed back the errant forelock. He guessed her age at about twenty-five. She was a head shorter than he, had black hair that fell in a girlish way to her shoulders. She had an artist's smock over her dress.

"How long has he been gone?"

"Not long." She looked at him curiously. "Would you like to wait for him?"

"Look," he said. "My name's Devan Traylor. I just got in from Florida to see how the project is getting along. I thought sure I'd find Dr. Costigan here. Where did he go?"

"Well..." She did not want to tell. "He's actually here, but not in this office. I'll get him for you if it's important. You say your name is Traylor. Is that right?"

"Right. But before you go, would you mind telling me where he is?"

"I'm sorry. I can't do that."

He did not press her for the information. Instead, he watched her take off her smock, put on a cardigan and start for the door. She looked very fetching in the sweater, he thought, and wondered who she was.

"I won't be a minute," she explained, her hand on the doorknob. She flashed him a smile and then, the roar from outside bursting in for a moment, she was gone.

He could have seen where she was going by watching her out the office window but he resisted the temptation. He only hoped she didn't have to go to a phone in some other office and get him out of a tavern.

In a few moments she was back. "It may take him a few minutes," she said. "But he'll be here." She took off the cardigan, put on the smock again.

"Does he have far to come?"

"Not far."

"You don't talk much, do you?"

"That depends."

"That is an admirable trait."

"What is?"

"To be able to speak when it's necessary and not when it isn't. What's your name?"

"Betty Peredge."

"You work for Dr. Costigan, apparently."

She nodded. "I've been here a month."

"Ever work for Inland before?"

"No. Mrs. Tudor, who was working for Dr. Costigan, became ill and he needed somebody for drafting in a hurry. I happened to be in the right place at the right time."

He saw for the first time two plants in flower pots in the window, one with a long, narrow leaf with yellow bands and without blossoms, and a violet plant, though he had not seen one with such fleshy leaves and large blossoms.

"Are those flowers yours or Mrs. Tudor's? I'm guessing they're not Dr. Costigan's."

"They're mine. I asked Dr. Costigan if I could bring them here. I happen to like flowers and they're something from home."

"What kind are they?"

"The one on the left is a sansevieria, sometimes called snake plant or mother-in-law's tongue, don't ask me why. The other I'm going to have to take home; it's doing poorly under this light. It's an African violet and you can see it's ailing. The leaves are yellow and the buds have been threatening to drop off."

He grinned. "I suppose it has a technical name, too?"

"Saintpaulia." She filled the ruling pen with ink, her tongue in her cheek, her hands steady.

"What do you think of the project, Miss Peredge?"

She put the stopper in the ink bottle, turned to him, a trace of amusement in her eyes. "I've become rather attached to Costigan's Needle," she said.

"Costigan's *Needle*?"

She nodded out the window to the floor of the big room. "You'll have to admit it will look like a needle with an eye at the bottom. You have the blue of an executive's badge. You ought to know what it's going to look like."

"I know, but I hadn't thought about it as a needle before." Twelve feet in diameter and more than sixty feet high—yes, with the inward taper on the bottom, that final eighteen feet drawing into a point at the top, it looked very much like a needle. Especially with a four by eight foot hole through the bottom as the needle's eye.

"Who named it that, Miss Peredge?"

"I don't know. I've heard it called nothing else. Even Dr. Costigan calls it the Needle."

"Are you his secretary or something?"

"In a way, yes. My most important work is making schematic drawings from his sketches so the electricians will have something to work from."

As she worked on her drawings, he walked to what he guessed was Dr. Costigan's desk. On top there were several large drawings of circuits she no doubt had made. He picked up the top three sheets and looked at them one at a time.

Three different circuit arrangements, all probably important, with a strange conglomeration of parts: banks of solenoids, time delay relays, voltage boosters, several rugged ceramic capacitors in one drawing, two focus coils and other devices in another, a deflection yoke and trivia in the third. He saw several insulated air-wound coils there, too, and almost laughed out loud. Who did Dr. Costigan think he was fooling?

He sat down, engrossed in following wires around in the top drawing. They went off the page and beneath them at the edge of the page, with an arrow pointing off the sheet, were the words *to box six*. He looked in vain for the diagram named *box six* and for that item on any other drawing.

"Look, Miss Peredge," he said, indicating the top drawing. She came over. "These wires here go to box number six, it says here. But there's no box number six drawing. Or is that what you're doing now?"

She shook her head. "I'm not doing it. On almost every drawing the wires go off to box numbers." She pointed to the box numbers on other sheets. "I haven't made a box number diagram in all the time I've been here." She paused. "Something else," she said. "I'm *Mrs.* Peredge."

"I'm sorry."

She looked at him sharply and he grinned. He was satisfied to let her take whichever meaning she wished.

"Do you know what the Needle is for, Mrs. Peredge?"

"Heavens no! But I've heard people talk about it. Some say it's a guided missile and others aren't sure. Do you know?"

"What do you think it is?"

"It doesn't seem to me it could be a guided missile. How would you get it out of here if it was? And all this preparation for just one of them—it wouldn't make sense. I think it must have something to do with atomic research, everything is so secret and the building is so closely guarded. Perhaps it's a cyclotron—a vertical one. They're usually round and flat, aren't they? I'm probably amusing you with my guesses. Have I come close?"

The rush of sound came in as the door opened.

"Mr. Traylor!" Dr. Costigan pumped his hand. "When did you get back?"

"Just today."

"This is certainly a surprise. I thought Mrs. Peredge said you were here, though it's hard to hear distinctly through that thick door. How is everything in Florida?" He arranged two folding chairs. "Sit down."

"Just fine, Doctor. How's everything up here?"

"You see, don't you? We're ahead of schedule. A couple more weeks and—well, we've got everything stockpiled around town ready to put in. It shouldn't be too long. A month at the outside."

"I'm glad to hear it."

"I was wondering when you'd get back. Didn't want you to miss the test. You'll be around for a while?"

"Couldn't keep me away. It's all I've been thinking about in Florida, to be frank."

"We've all been thinking about nothing else, I guess."

"Where's Sam?"

Dr. Costigan wiped his watery eyes with his handkerchief. "We put Sam in purchasing. He's happy there and he's doing a good job. They tell me Sam gets material that's impossible to get. He's out on a buying errand right now."

"And Orcutt?"

"He doesn't get out here much. He and Basher, Holcombe, Tooksberry and—"

"Tooksberry? Does he come nosing around?"

"He doesn't like what we're doing, but he comes out to have a look once in a while. He and I just don't get along, Mr. Traylor."

"We don't either." Devan offered him a cigarette, not remembering whether or not the doctor smoked.

Dr. Costigan shook his head. "What's this door you mentioned, Doctor? The one you said is so thick."

"Well..." The doctor gave him a sidelong glance. "I hope you weren't too set on those plans of yours. I did a little changing. This is my office, really, just as you said, but I've built another office down at the end of this line of offices. We chopped a few feet off each office so I could have it. Did you notice it when you came in? My workshop is in there. It's more private."

Devan studied his face. "Why do you need a workshop? You have this whole building, haven't you?"

"Yes, but—" The doctor was having difficulty. "You see, there are some boxes to be put in the Needle."

"Needle? We called it a tube before."

"I don't know how it started, but suddenly everybody was calling it that. Anyway, there are several vital parts of the Needle I'm building myself. If I didn't, the secret would be easily revealed."

Devan picked up the diagrams he'd been examining. "That's what you mean here, eh? 'To box six.' That's one of those boxes you're working on, is that right?"

"Yes. There are to be ten of them."

"Ten vital spots." Devan fingered the charts. "Tell me, do all these things work you have indicated here—relays, focus coils, deflection yokes?"

The doctor smiled. "Well, some do and some don't. I run all the wires to the boxes and just connect the ones that run to equipment to be used. A safety precaution."

"Sounds like diverting tactics to me. You say it will be ready in a couple weeks, Doctor?"

Dr. Costigan glanced at Betty Peredge.

"I've seen that look before," she said, smiling and rising from her work. "I know when I'm not wanted." She exchanged her smock for a sweater again and left the room.

There was much about the girl Devan liked. He decided she wasn't what he'd call pictorially beautiful, but she was beautiful by animation, especially when that smile was aimed at him... and then he remembered she was married and so was he and so he tried to get his mind off her blue cardigan.

"I mentioned something about the Needle being ready in two weeks," Devan reminded the doctor.

Dr. Costigan leaned closer to him. "There is a problem."

"A problem?"

"Yes. Evidently nobody's thought about who is to go through the Needle's Eye first. Have you?"

5

The giant chamber echoed every movement, every scrape of a shoe, even the scratch of a paper match one of them struck to light a cigarette. The six men sat in a small group near the Eye of the Needle, while the seventh man worked. They sat close to each other as if for warmth or safety, though the real reason was easier communication. When they talked, they did so softly.

It was the night of the big test.

Orcutt sat with his legs crossed, one foot moving slowly up and down, a forefinger curved around the stem of the pipe in his mouth, his eyes on Dr. Costigan, who had removed a plate from the polished metal side of the Needle and was working with wires inside.

Sam Otto, Glenn Basher and Howard Tooksberry were having lively discussions about a variety of subjects—the weather, the stock market, the international situation and football—though Devan thought April was an odd month to be talking about football. James Holcombe didn't enter into the talk much. He kept fidgeting in his chair, cracking his knuckles and watching the doctor.

Workmen had completed the Needle in the middle of April. Since then Dr. Costigan had been promising the executive committee a demonstration. It had taken a few days to install the secret boxes. Then had come the tests. Never the Needle itself, always some circuit that the doctor wanted to balance just right.

He'd work from point to point with the test probes, volt-ohmmeters, signal generators, videometers and some testing devices that looked homemade to Devan. They were in small plywood boxes with the usual meters on the outside. One of the boxes was equipped with a headphone set and the physicist walked around with the phones, making adjustments with a knob on the box and recording figures on a pad. It could have been a Geiger counter, except it wasn't.

Just to make sure, Devan borrowed a Geiger counter from Inland's big supply room, made a test circle of the Needle with it himself, got nothing out of the ordinary in the neon flasher or earphones or on the milliroentgen scale. So much for that. There were no gamma rays, X-rays, radioactive ores or cosmic rays in the tube. Whatever Dr. Costigan was testing for, Devan could not guess.

The executive committee had been informed that afternoon that the first test was to be made that night. The seven of them had met at seven o'clock in the big room, moved chairs close to the Needle. That seemed days ago to Devan. The doctor had slowed things to a crawl.

First, Dr. Costigan had moved a large control panel on a pedestal across the floor on rubber tires to one side of the Eye, a large rubber-covered cable running from the portable panel to a bank of control panels along the wall.

Then he had punched a red button at the top of the panel and instantly there was a loud hum of several motors and a final *clang* that resounded in the room. Then there was silence. Devan could see the red lights over the big electrically operated doors, knew then that no one could get in or out. Even the guard in the small office adjacent to the big doors could not enter the experimental room.

But what happened when the red button was pushed was the only thing of any real interest that had happened for over an hour. Dr. Costigan had started operations, pushing buttons, pulling levers this way and that and swearing slightly when things evidently didn't add up right on his panel. He switched everything off, had been working on the Needle's wiring ever since. Nobody offered to help; the doctor discouraged it. So the six of them sat back, variously occupied, while the thin scientist, bent over the small opening to one side of the Needle's Eye, pushed and prodded and grunted and swore.

The Needle was a beautiful shaft of gleaming metal that rose from the floor, its surface unbroken except for an occasional eye bolt from which guy wires ran to the wall. It looked capable of anything and Devan presumed that it probably had been considered for a number of things in the conjectures of those who had worked on it so feverishly in the past two months. The wires that bound it to the walls made it look like a landlocked guided missile.

He saw Dr. Costigan step back, put his hands to the small of his back and straighten, grimacing as he did so. Then he picked up the metal panel, put it back into place, screwed it tight, then walked stiffly over to the control pedestal and flicked a few switches. The doctor's face brightened.

"Ah," he said, eyes darting here and there around the panel's many dials, "I think that's it." He looked up. "I think we're ready."

As had been planned, Sam Otto moved from his chair to a small box near by. Orcutt moved a U-shaped wooden enclosure to the Eye of the Needle. Sam picked a large, white rabbit out of the box, dropped it into the small yard made by the low fence.

"All right, Bugs," he said. "On your way."

They all crowded around, watched the rabbit's pink nose exploring the concrete floor, then the air. He did not move toward the Eye.

"You ought to have a carrot to lure him," Devan said.

"I've got one," Sam said, moving his cigar around with his teeth and lips. "I almost forgot." He withdrew a carrot from his pocket, broke it into several pieces, tossed them into the Eye area where they rolled along the floor. "I hope Hodge's Grocery has the kind of carrots rabbits like."

At first the rabbit did nothing, then his nose went into the air and he wiggled the end of it. Suddenly he hunched and jumped, hunched and jumped again. He paused, sniffed the air, seemed certain he was headed right, hopped quickly into the Needle's Eye and disappeared from view. The carrot pieces were still there.

For a long time they stood there, watching the area underneath the Needle, the archway Eye, four feet wide and eight feet high, twelve feet deep at the top and only eight feet deep at the bottom because of the tapering sides of the Needle at the floor. The Eye looked deceptively safe.

The rabbit did not come out.

"He could come out the other side, couldn't he?" Basher asked.

"I should think so," Holcombe said. "He goes along the concrete here, then he comes to the Needle's Eye, goes into it, disappears from us, doesn't find the carrot pieces because they're here and not where he is. He's bound to come out one side or the other."

"Maybe he can't find his way out," Tooksberry said. "Maybe he's as confused as we are."

"I've kept the power on," Dr. Costigan said. "I should think he'd find his way out. First he smelled the carrots, started after them. When he didn't find them I should think he'd think they are farther on and come out on the other side looking for them."

"Nothing's come out," Sam said. "Let's try the other one."

"Might as well."

The same thing happened to the second rabbit.

"Look," Orcutt said, finally. "This business with animals tells us it works. That's fine. But does it tell us anything else? What we need to do is walk in there ourselves and see what it's like."

"Just a minute," Dr. Costigan said. "That would be risky, don't you think? Suppose we all go in and none of us comes out? Who's left to tell what went on here?"

"Oh, hell," Orcutt said. "We're different from a damn rabbit. We have brains. We'd mark the spot and come through it when we wanted to come back."

"Think so?" The doctor was smiling. "Remember my first experiments? My arms met water. I was in a basement and when my arm went through the hole, it encountered water. Suppose the same thing happens here? What if you came out in water?"

"Then you'd go up to the top, if you didn't drown on the way," Orcutt said. "I see your point, though. But there's no sense in standing here." He started for the Eye.

"Wait, Ed." Devan was on his feet. "What are you going to do?"

"Just feel if there's water, Dev. That's all." He moved the wooden enclosure away and they all crowded around the opening.

It looked innocent, that area just within the lips of the Eye. As Devan approached it, he had a fleeting impulse to jump into it, such as he had experienced when he was high in a building and felt like jumping to the street. He supposed many people felt that way and, as he observed the curious, tense faces of those about the Eye, wondered if any of them was controlling an urge to fall into the Eye.

Orcutt moved closer than the rest. "No pushing, boys," he said. There was a laugh and tension lowered.

He thrust his hand into the Eye. It disappeared. He moved his invisible hand down.

"Pretty chilly," he said. "But no water."

His hand went to the floor — and lower.

"We're on the ground, aren't we?" he asked in some surprise.

"Yes, Ed," Devan said. "We excavated a little underneath the wooden floor of the old factory so we'd be on ground level."

"Well, my hand goes down quite away..."

Suddenly he withdrew his hand, stood up. "This is ridiculous. I'm going through the Eye — all of me." He turned to go in it.

"Now, wait," Dr. Costigan said.

Orcutt hesitated.

"I invented this thing," Dr. Costigan went on. "Don't you think I should have the honor of going through the Eye first?"

"But we don't know what's on the other side," Devan protested. "After all, you're not as young as Ed here, Doctor."

"You're the inventor," Basher said. "You'd better stay here, don't you think?"

"Frankly, no," the doctor said coolly.

"You may have invented the Needle," Orcutt said, "but it was I who swung the board to thinking we ought to invest in it."

"What about me?" Sam said, smiling cherubically. "Where would any of you be if it weren't for my offering Dr. Costigan's idea to you?" He moved forward. "One side, gentlemen. Let me through. I want to feel like Columbus." It didn't take much to restrain him, just the merest pressure on his arm by the doctor. "Well, I tried."

"How about Jimmy?" Devan said. "He's president of the board. Maybe he ought to go first."

"Maybe you all ought to go," Tooksberry said, drawing back from them. "You could get on your marks, get set and run from a distance and the first one through is 'it.' And after you've all gone through, I could turn the machine off."

"Very funny," Orcutt said. "Well, we're getting nothing done this way."

"There's a fair way," Sam said. "We could draw straws."

"I'll agree to that," the doctor said.

The others approved the move—everybody but Tooksberry.

"I'll get the straws," he said. "I'll arrange them. I don't want one myself." He went off to search for a broom. When he came back he had six straws in his hand. "Take your pick, gentlemen."

It had not been Devan's intention to volunteer to go through the Needle's Eye, but someone was going to have to go and the more he got to thinking about it, the more the idea of his going appealed to him. The area just beyond that brightly illuminated doorway held the secret to what had been puzzling them all since they had seen the first Needle. Perhaps Sam Otto wasn't so far wrong; going through the Needle's Eye might be equivalent to Columbus's voyage across the Atlantic. Perhaps the name of the first man to pass through the Eye would become a household word for all the years to come. It depended, of course, upon the significance of what lay on the other side. But Devan wasn't concerned with the significance of it at the moment; he was moved more by curiosity. He drew an offered straw.

Glenn Basher held the short straw high. "I've got it."

He moved to the Eye opening and then turned toward them. "I think this is the only way, just as Orcutt says." He smiled a little nervously, lit a cigarette. "But I'd like to try a few things I've thought of, first."

"Go ahead," Orcutt said. "It's your party. You won the short straw. But if you don't want to go, I'll take your place."

Basher shook his head. "No. I've been wondering a long time about it and now I'm glad I won't have to hear about it from anybody else. I can go myself." He took a deep drag on the cigarette, crushed it out under foot. Then he lay down on the concrete floor, moved himself toward the Eye as if he were stealing through underbrush. At last he had only a few inches to go before his head would be inside the entranceway.

"Here goes!" he said. He lunged forward, stuck his head into the Eye. His head disappeared. Several small pieces of metal dropped to the concrete floor.

After several minutes Basher's head was out again and he got to his feet. "It's chilly in there. I could feel a breeze. But I didn't see a damn thing. Got to walk into it, I guess." He stopped talking, his face went blank and he was doing something with his mouth.

"I'll be damned!" He worked his mouth around, his tongue poking his cheek out here and there. "All my fillings are gone!"

The others walked to the Eye entranceway, saw the metal fillings on the concrete.

"The Eye won't pass inanimate objects," Dr. Costigan said.

Basher stooped to pick up his fillings, his hand disappearing as he did so. Suddenly he lost his balance and started to fall forward, uttering a cry.

A dozen hands reached for him, a few caught his clothes... and held them.

His clothes were there. But they were limp and empty.

All of Glenn Basher had gone through the Eye. He had completely disappeared.

For a few moments they all stood quiet and unmoving. They knew Basher was going to go through the Eye but they had expected him to do it in an orderly manner. They had expected him to step through, stay a few minutes and then step back and report. Then, if everything seemed all right, he would go through for a longer period. If this worked well, then they could all go through to see what it was like.

As it was, Basher's falling through the Eye jarred them as nothing else had that evening and the echo of his cry still rang in their ears.

Sam Otto was the first to move. He was looking toward the opening as if it were a thing of horror, lips moving, jaw working, face white. Then he started to move away from the opening slowly.

Orcutt saw him. "Let's not lose our heads, gentle-men," he said moving over and taking Sam's arm. "Let's examine the facts."

They sat down and Sam seemed to come out of it, starting to wipe cold sweat from his forehead with his handkerchief.

"We have Glenn's clothes," Orcutt said. "That means he is in there naked, so he won't want to be in there long. He has more sense than our rabbits. He'll find his way out. All we have to do is sit here and wait."

They were quiet and sat without exchanging a word for a long time. Orcutt started his pipe; Holcombe and Devan lit cigarettes. Sam Otto retrieved the cigar that had fallen out of his mouth during the tussle with Basher and, to Devan's amazement, put a match to it. Only Dr. Costigan remained standing, examining the dials on the portable control panel.

As the time dragged slowly on, Devan grew increas-ingly uneasy. Both Orcutt and Basher had remarked on how cold it was in the Eye, and Basher, without clothes, wouldn't want to stay there long. He remem-bered that Orcutt's hand had gone beneath the con-crete and hadn't touched anything. Was there anything to touch? How far was down?

Orcutt's hand hadn't gone into outer space, that was certain; otherwise the chill of it and the absence of air would have done damage. But where did the hand go? In Dr. Costigan's experiment in his first basement, the Needle's Eye had opened into water. Nothing inor-ganic could be transferred through the Eye, so the wa-ter did not come through to the basement. In the ex-

periment in his second basement, the Eye opened out
to air—above water, he presumed, since air wouldn't
be under water. On the second floor of the factory the
hole had opened to cold air, air as cold as that outside
at the time. The water and the cold air proved the Eye
opened to a world just like this one, didn't it? They had
been over that: forward or backward in time, perhaps,
or another area on the earth itself.

The bottom of the Needle was at ground level. Why
hadn't Orcutt's hand touched ground in the other area?
But then that wasn't reasonable—there was no water in
the basement where the doctor had performed his first
experiment, so why should there be ground here now?
Unless it was an underground water supply in this
other place, assuming once again this other place was
just like this one... Thinking about it made his head
swim.

"Basher's dead."

The sudden words that shook them all out of their
reveries and made Devan jump were uttered by
Tooksberry.

"That's a hell of a thing to say," Orcutt said.

"Why doesn't he come back, then?" Tooksberry's
eyes were triumphant. "Dead things don't come back
from the other side."

"Basher's not dead!" Holcombe snapped a little too
quickly.

"He hasn't come back, though."

"Listen, you!" Sam was pale. "You shut up talk like
that!"

Tooksberry grunted and leered at him.

"Somebody's got to go after Glenn," Orcutt said. "And I'm nominating myself."

"No, Ed." Devan got to his feet. "None of us is going after him. I've thought of that. So have the others, I'm sure. We've got to stay here, all of us. Otherwise we'll all be moving through the Needle's Eye one at a time and there won't be anybody left."

"Except me," Tooksberry said. "You'll never get me in that thing."

"Maybe somebody ought to shove you in it," Sam said.

"Well," Orcutt said, ignoring Sam, "maybe you're right, Dev. But I'm going to stick my head in. As Basher did."

"Ready to lose your fillings?"

"I don't give a damn. Basher's more important. I can always get new fillings."

Orcutt lay down on the floor, Devan holding one leg, Holcombe holding the other. They moved him slowly toward the opening. He raised his head as he neared it, his hands on the side of the opening, the fingers disappearing into the Eye.

"Just like a ledge," he said, fascinated with the way the backs of his hands were visible and his fingers were not. "Ready? Here goes!"

He moved his head forward into the empty space and it disappeared. There was a rattle of metal particles as his dental fillings hit the floor. He stayed that way for a long time, moving a little once in a while, Devan and Holcombe never releasing their grip on his legs. Finally, his head came out. His face was despair itself.

"No sign of him. It's cold and dark and damp in there." Orcutt's white hair was disheveled and his manner was discouraged. "I tried to sense everything I could. Just a stiff breeze for movement and only the vaguest grays for light. No idea where the ground is, if there is any. I yelled for Basher but I didn't get any answer. I didn't even hear an echo."

Four hours later six glum men sent for Mrs. Basher.

She lived in Wilmette and by the time she came by taxicab, early-morning April mist was lifting from everything and dull grays were bringing Chicago buildings into sharp relief against the sky.

Devan remembered her as a shy young thing. Basher had introduced her around the office when she had come up one day, but no one at Inland had ever become acquainted with her; the Bashers seemed to prefer their own company.

He had forgotten she had red hair. Now the hair was much in evidence as were the question marks in her eyes as the six of them tried to tell her what happened, explaining how much of a secret it all was, how Basher had chosen the short straw, how he had wanted to go.

She didn't believe a word of it. And to make matters worse, when Orcutt tried to show her how his hand could disappear in the Needle's Eye, it didn't disappear.

This sent Dr. Costigan into a flurry of examining all the dials, of checking the connections. Finally, he had to turn it all off to check the repairs he had made earlier that night.

Mrs. Basher, breathing more rapidly as she became more angry, her eyes beginning to narrow and fill with deep suspicion as each man tried to explain in his own way, suddenly turned on her heel and walked to the door. She couldn't get it open because it wouldn't open unless Dr. Costigan punched the proper button on the control panel. When Devan tried to take advantage of her forced delay and explain it all over again, she slapped him soundly.

"You open that door, do you hear!"

"But why? Don't you believe us?"

"No. Something's happened to Glenn and you're trying to... to... Open that door!"

"What are you going to do?"

"Tell the police. They'll get the truth out of you!"

Devan grabbed her and shook her. This only made Mrs. Basher's eyes blaze all the more furiously. She wrested herself from him.

"Don't you dare touch me!" she said, outraged.

"But you can't tell the police!"

"Oh, can't I?"

"But that would spoil everything!"

"Then tell the truth about my husband. Do you think I'm fool enough to fall for this-this fairy tale you're telling?"

"But it's the truth!"

Orcutt came up. "He's right, Mrs. Basher."

"Open this door!"

Devan shrugged. He looked toward Dr. Costigan who was at the control panel and nodded to him. The red light above the door winked out.

"You can go through the door now, Mrs. Basher," he said.

"Telling the police will get you nothing," Orcutt said.

The door shut.

6

If the gloom that had descended upon the six men remaining in the big Needle chamber had been three dimensional, it could not have seemed more real. When Mrs. Basher stepped through the door to get the police, they were all shocked and each man suddenly got busy examining his conscience and, thankfully, found it unsullied.

Still, they were very distressed and Devan found them looking so distraught when he turned from the door that he could not help breaking into a laugh, albeit a rather hysterical laugh.

"What the hell is there to laugh about?" Sam Otto said. "She just wrecked the project."

"I don't think so," Devan said. "I don't think we need worry too much. What can she prove?"

"But she'll tell the police what the Needle will do," Dr. Costigan said. "Then the secret will be out."

"All that publicity we could use later," Sam said. "It would ruin us now."

Devan shook his head. "Which one of us believed in the Needle when he first heard about it? I know I didn't. Remember how each of you felt? No, I think the police will think she's insane. She'll probably insist and after a while, since she'll tell the same story over and over again the same way, they'll send somebody out."

"But that's really the last thing we want, isn't it?" Orcutt said. "People nosing around the Needle?"

"It needn't be fatal. I don't think any of us saw Basher go through the Needle's Eye, did we? He just suddenly walked off without telling us, that's all—if you know what I mean. And though each of us, off the record, did see him disappear in the Eye, we can't prove it, can we? First of all, the Needle's not working at the moment. Second, where is his body? You can't prove anything these days without a body, can you? If we all stand pat, the police will leave quickly, I think."

Sam Otto smiled. "I see what you mean, Devan. There can't be a crime without the corpus delicti you always hear about in the murder mysteries. Maybe they'll put Mrs. Basher in the booby hatch."

"I don't know about that. But I do know they'll investigate. We'll have to put Basher's clothes in Dr. Costigan's workshop and admit nothing except the truth: Glenn Basher has disappeared. Maybe we think he's vanished in the hole, but we're not certain, in case your conscience bothers you."

Tooksberry nodded his head. "That may be very sensible. But it still doesn't bring Glenn back."

"If we all go to jail we'll never get him back."

"You fellows figure it all out," Dr. Costigan said. "I've got to get the Needle working again. Mr. Basher might even now be looking for the way back."

It wasn't more than an hour later that Detective Sergeant Walter Peavine and Detective Timothy Griffin arrived to begin their investigation. The sergeant, a large man with a thick neck, a burr haircut and protruding brown eyes, got to the point at once and seemed peeved that no one would say the missing man was missing through the courtesy, or discourtesy, of Costigan's Needle. Detective Griffin devoted his time to a studied tour of the building.

The detective sergeant tried a number of ways of extracting information from them all and failed, always coming back with another method not quite as courteous and gentlemanly as the previous one until Orcutt could stand it no longer.

"Sergeant, let me ask *you* a question," Orcutt said, hands behind his back, balancing on the balls of his feet and glaring at the policeman as if he had been insulted. "Tell me frankly, would you believe it if I told you Glenn Basher walked into that opening and disappeared?"

Detective Sergeant Peavine inspected the Needle with a respectful eye. "Of course not. You think I'm crazy?"

"Then why are you asking us if he did?"

The plain-clothes man was fascinated by the beauty, line and symmetry of the Needle. He could hardly tear his eyes away from it.

"All right," the sergeant said. "I admit it's crazy, but we have to check on these things, you know. Mrs. Basher came into the precinct station and raised hell, telling us you tried to hand her a story about her husband walking into a hole and disappearing."

"How *is* Mrs. Basher, Sergeant?" Devan asked. "Is she resting well? She was pretty upset when she was here."

"She was feeling pretty good when we left. She was fit to be tied when she came in, though. Don't think I've ever seen a woman as angry." He coughed. "But to get back to the business of her husband... Some one of you called her and told her to come down. Isn't that right?"

"That's right, Sergeant," Holcombe said. "It so happens that Glenn Basher did duck out right in the middle of an experiment and we... well"—he smiled embarrassedly—"we wondered if he went on home."

"Here one minute," Sam said, snapping his fingers, "and gone the next. We were hoping she could give us a clue. Very mysterious."

"Classic puzzle, isn't it?" the sergeant said drily. "All the doors and windows locked, ventilators closed, and so on. Yet someone disappears."

"That's right, Inspector," Tooksberry said.

Sergeant Peavine looked at Tooksberry. "It's *sergeant.*"

"Of course. Sorry."

Cleated shoes beat a tattoo as the other detective came across the floor. "I've looked through everything, Sergeant. Found nothing except a few locked rooms."

"We'll get to those, Tim. Stick around." The sergeant deftly spun a chair around and sat facing the back of it. He looked at the six of them and then looked at the Needle. "What are you fellows doing here at this time of the morning, anyway?"

"I told you, Sergeant," Orcutt said, rubbing the stubble on his chin. "Force field experiments."

"My kid would like to see that." The sergeant pointed to the Needle.

"Bring him down."

"He's nuts about space travel. Could tell you the size and distance of every planet." He turned to Orcutt. "How much do you weigh?"

"One hundred and eighty-five pounds. Why?"

"On the planet Mars," the sergeant said, "you'd weigh only two-fifths that much. Randolph, that's my boy, could figure it out for you. A two hundred pound man would weigh only eighty pounds. That will give you an idea of some of the conditions on Mars. Amazing, isn't it?"

"This isn't a space ship, Sergeant."

"Think how easy it would be to hit a home run on Mars! Wouldn't the boys in the outfield be really *out!* Think of the size of the baseball park!"

"I say, Sergeant. You're on the wrong track. This isn't a space ship."

"It isn't?" The detective was disappointed. "Sure looks like one. What is it?"

"Well, as near as we can figure out," Orcutt said, passing a quick glance Devan's way, "it's a problem."

"I suppose that's a wisecrack."

"No. I mean it has handed us a problem in hyperspace and its relationship to the space around us."

"At the moment," Devan put in, "we're worried about the transferability of living cellular structures from here to there and back again. Particularly the return."

"That's right, Sergeant," Sam Otto said.

"Yeah, yeah." The sergeant pulled a cigarette from a pack, stuck it in his mouth. "Who's the old duck over there with the wires?"

"That's Dr. Winfield Costigan," Orcutt said. "He invented the Needle."

This was getting nowhere, Devan decided. He looked at his watch. Seven o'clock. In another hour people would start reporting for work. What then?

"I don't get it," the sergeant said. "You build something and don't even know what it does or how it works."

"Would you like to meet the inventor?" Devan asked.

The sergeant nodded, two jets of smoke emanating from his nostrils, a hint of awe in his eyes as he followed Devan closely. Detective Griffin kept with them.

"This is Sergeant Peavine of the detective bureau," Devan said.

The physicist grunted, twirled a knob, watched a dial.

"That's Dr. Costigan."

"Having trouble?" the sergeant asked.

Dr. Costigan looked up. "Yes." He walked from the control box to the opening in the hull of the Needle, withdrew a cable of wires, inspected a wiring diagram on a stool at his side.

"Won't it work?"

"Not now."

"What does it do when it works?"

"Haven't quite decided yet. It's never worked that good yet." The doctor squinted at the diagram. "Would you mind handing me that chart for a moment, please?"

The sergeant picked up the diagram, handed it to the doctor.

"How will you know when it works, then?"

"That's it!" The doctor let the chart fall to the floor. "Hold this." He handed the sergeant a trouble light. The sergeant held it aloft, got on his tiptoes to see what the doctor was doing. "Ah!" Dr. Costigan sighed. "That's more like it! Correct resistance now in that circuit. Sure a funny thing what a few ohms more or less will do to unbalance a circuit." He moved past the sergeant, leaving him with the light. The detective finally turned it off and put it on the stool.

The sergeant then moved and tried to see the top of the Needle from the floor, a feat that Devan could have told him was impossible. While the sergeant craned his neck, Devan glanced at the doctor, then looked casually around to see Detective Griffin walking toward them from around the Needle.

"Sure is a big thing," the sergeant said. "Just like pictures in Randolph's books."

"Listen to this," Griffin said, rapping his knuckles against the side of the Needle. The sound was a hollow one. Detective Griffin came nearer, tapping as he came. He looked at the archway. "What's this?"

Griffin stooped to examine the fillings a little more closely.

Dr. Costigan yelled "Hey!"

Everybody looked at Dr. Costigan, then, seeing the horror on his face, turned back to look at the plain-clothes man.

Griffin, startled by the voice and the doctor's expression, had taken a step backward and met with no resistance because the step took him into the Eye of the Needle.

While everyone watched, the detective's rearmost foot met nothing. His face filled with astonishment and the yell he started as he fell backward was cut off when his head disappeared.

The hands that reached for support met only empty air and the clutching fingers and arms themselves vanished from the sleeves as they entered the Eye area. His suit crumpled to the concrete floor, empty. The movement of the shoes into the Eye sent them part way through and they stopped in a grotesque position, toes pointing at each other, shoelaces still tied, socks draped over the sides.

It seemed as if the seconds were minutes. They were long moments of agony. Devan sensed that the nerves of them all tightened as if the invisible web in which they were all caught had suddenly become energized and was drawing taut....

"Tim," came the whisper from his side. Sergeant Peavine, his face a pasty white, the fingers of the hands at his sides flexing spasmodically, stared stupefied.

"Timmy!" The sergeant became a man of action suddenly. He moved toward the Needle's Eye. "TIMOTHY!"

Devan expected the sergeant to disappear when he went into the Eye but he did not. The doctor had shut off the machine.

They all rushed close now and saw the sergeant on the floor inside the archway, his hands patting the missing detective's clothes as if he expected some part of the man to be still within it.

He picked up the coat and then the shoes, then let them fall and picked up the other clothing. A pink and white object rolled out from the clothes and the plain-clothes man picked it up and stared at it.

"I'll be damned," he said. "Griffin's upper plate!"

7

The scheme to keep the function of the Needle a secret exploded with force. Detective Sergeant Peavine started the chain reaction, with Devan, Orcutt, Sam Otto, Holcombe, Tooksberry and Dr. Costigan the next step in the reaction: they gave information about the Needle to uniformed men who told newsmen who told the public who wanted to know more and told the newsmen and the newsmen came back and went now directly to the men who had seen the two men disappear and asked more questions.

It was a nightmare. Things had passed so suddenly out of the hands of the tight little research group that it hardly seemed real. They were all haggard, worn, unshaven and hungry but the police department had ordered that they were not to leave the building. There were reporters and photographers and radiomen and policemen everywhere and as each new one came in, he paused for a few moments to look at the Needle, then came up to the group around the six research men.

"Is this really on the level, Mac?"

"Costigan's Needle? What's it for?"

"You say he disappeared in *there?*"

"Can you or do you know anyone who can explain this?"

"Would you mind starting at the beginning again?"

New faces every minute demanding to know, new pencils poised to write on new pads, in new notebooks, people shoving their faces forward, some with badges, others without, people quiet and retiring, merely observing and reporting and smiling and frowning.

And then the pictures. Pictures inside and outside the Eye. Official and unofficial photos. Newspaper and police. Photographs of them separately and together, some candid shots using only the light of the big room itself, others with every manner of flash bulb, photoflash unit, special bulbs for color, every kind and type of exposure sometimes using the police and sometimes not, with and without the clothing of Detective Griffin and Glenn Basher.

"One more, please."

"Hold it right there. That's right. Now just one more."

"A little to the left. There."

"Just one more, please. Hold it."

Devan felt faint with hunger. He had run out of everything, cigarettes, stamina and patience, and his eyelids felt as if someone were sitting on them. He knew the others felt as he did, knew they were as disgusted as he was with the answers they got from the police when they asked them for a chance to have breakfast sent in.

"You'll get breakfast as soon as we're through with this preliminary part of the investigation," they were told by Lieutenant Harold Johnson, a large, blond, heavy-set man who filled out his uniform the way a police officer should.

It was Betty Peredge who helped out. She came to work at nine, wouldn't be stopped by the police guard at the research room door and demanded to know what they were doing to her boss. She refused to answer questions and, by plunge and feint, finally made her way over to the besieged six men.

Not knowing who or what she was, the ring of men broke to let her in.

"What are they doing to you?" she asked, coming through to them. "I've been listening on the radio." Then she saw Dr. Costigan. "Oh, Doctor! You look all in! Can't I do something for you?"

"Just bring me a gallon of coffee, a double order of ham and eggs and a bed, Mrs. Peredge," he said. "That's all I need."

Betty turned angrily to the policemen. "What's the matter with you officers? Can't you see these men need a rest? They've been awake all night. How would you feel if someone kept hounding you with questions if you were dead on your feet?"

The officers moved back a little, leaving Lieutenant Johnson an island to face her. He walked to her. "Lady," he said. "I don't know who you are, but you haven't any business here."

There were a few chuckles at this. Betty's dark blue eyes flashed. "I have every right in the world here. I happen to be Dr. Costigan's assistant. I don't know who you are."

"I'm Lieutenant Johnson, in charge of this detail. I'm asking you like a gentleman to leave these men alone."

"If you were a gentleman you'd have seen to it that they had something to eat."

"The department will take care of it. All in good time."

"They're mighty slow getting around to it, I'd say. What kind of a police department does Chicago have? It ought to be obvious these men haven't had a bit of anything to eat since their dinner last night, that they haven't had a minute's sleep, that they haven't had a chance to shave."

"Lady—" The lieutenant's face was red.

"I'm not a lady. I'm Mrs. Peredge," Betty said. "I work here and I know these men and I'm going to order their breakfasts."

"Lady—" The lieutenant's face was redder. Then suddenly it turned white and his resistance crumbled. "All right," he said. "All right, men. We'll take a break. Let's give these fellows some air. We'll continue the questions after they have their breakfasts."

They felt better after breakfast in Dr. Costigan's office and after they all had made use of Dr. Costigan's electric razor.

"This is more like it!" Dr. Costigan said, patting his stomach expansively. "I'll admit it's a little early in the morning, but I think a spot of brandy would make it just about perfect." He looked out of the office window at the milling people.

Devan lit a cigarette from a package purchased for him by Betty and inhaled it gratefully. Orcutt filled his pipe. Sam Otto was munching on the last piece of toast.

"You're supposed to meet over at the Needle," Betty said, coming in from the outside. "Just talked to the lieutenant. He wants to see a demonstration of the machine."

"Just as long as there are no more questions!" Dr. Costigan said.

"Don't say that," Sam Otto said, his eyes bright and the cigar Betty had thoughtfully provided lolling out of his mouth. "This publicity ought to make us."

"At the expense of Glenn Basher and the detective," Tooksberry said. "They will prevent any more experiments with the Needle when they see how it works. They'll probably close this place up."

Sam shook his head. "No they won't. You don't know what publicity can do. People won't rest now till they know what's in the Needle's Eye. There'll be too much public pressure to bring back the detective to close the Needle down. Somebody's going to have to go into the Eye and bring back the right answer. You just wait and see."

"I'm sorry it was ever started," Orcutt said wearily. "If I had known it was going to cost the lives of two men..."

"Nonsense!" Devan said. "We don't know that Basher and Griffin are dead. We'll never know until someone goes in there and comes back."

Policemen, newsmen, photographers, investigators, the six Inland Electronics men and Betty Peredge assembled at the Needle's Eye where the six explained in detail just what had happened to the two men, Sergeant Peavine corroborating the part about Detective Griffin.

"The machine ought to be on now," Orcutt said. "Our man, Mr. Basher, and your man, Mr. Griffin, may right now be trying to find the way back. They'll never do it if the Needle isn't on."

"I want a demonstration," the lieutenant said, "but I don't want any more fatalities."

"Fatalities!" Sam Otto snorted.

"You'll all have to move back, away from the machine," the lieutenant ordered. "Then we'll have the test."

They moved away from the Eye and Dr. Costigan set the switches and adjusted dials and turned it on. "It's working," he said from the portable panel.

Lieutenant Johnson gave him a dubious look, glared at Sergeant Peavine. "It looks the same as it did before."

"Of course," Dr. Costigan said. "Put your hand in the Eye there and you'll see what happens. Be careful, though."

The lieutenant moved cautiously to the Eye, his hands in front of him. He got close, saw the ends of his fingers disappear. The crowd gasped. He drew his hands back quickly, rubbed them together. He put out trembling hands again experimentally, saw the same thing happen, drew them back even more quickly, looked at them and saw they were whole.

"All right," he said, dropping his hands to his sides. "Turn it off." He stared at the Eye unbelievingly.

"Wait a minute," Devan said. "You can't shut off the machine now."

"Why not?"

"It's just as Mr. Orcutt says, Lieutenant. Detective Griffin and Glenn Basher may be looking for a way back from wherever they are. They can only return here if the machine is working."

"You think they're alive?"

"Your hands aren't dead, are they?"

"Well..."

"There is a better way, a quicker way to find out where they are."

"What's that?"

"Someone could go in the Eye and show them the way back."

The lieutenant shook his head. "No one is going into that Eye and that's final. As a matter of fact, if the machine stays on it constitutes a menace. Someone else is apt to fall in."

"Believe me, Lieutenant," Orcutt said, "it's the *only* way to get your detective back. If you turn it off you're sentencing him to his permanent absence from this life."

It took a lot of convincing. The lieutenant finally checked with the chief of police who, it was rumored, checked with the commissioner who checked with the mayor before it was decided the Eye should stay open to the other side. As a precaution, a fence was ordered built around the Needle, a wooden fence seven feet high, a fence with a gate and a policeman at the gate facing the Needle's Eye. No one was to go into the enclosure and the policeman was to keep his eye on the

Eye to give the word at the first sight of anybody or *anything*. He was armed.

"I don't see why they couldn't have let you go," Betty said as workmen were building the ordered fence early in the afternoon. She was sitting with Devan on an empty packing case in front of Dr. Costigan's office; their backs were against the front wall of the office.

"They keep hoping we'll produce Detective Griffin like a rabbit out of a hat," Devan said.

"From what was said, he could come walking out of the Eye. Is that right?"

"Yes. That's possible."

"The Needle is certainly remarkable."

"That's the word for it, all right. But we've known for months what it will do."

"If you knew, why did you have to build it? It doesn't seem to really accomplish anything except making people disappear."

"I'll agree. It's only got us in trouble so far."

"It's stirred up Chicago and the rest of the country. Do you realize there's very little else on the radio?"

"I suppose."

"In the papers, too, I imagine, from all the pictures they have taken." She contemplated the tall, stately Needle. "To think some of the circuits I put on drafting paper are now part of that big thing. But surely there must have been some other reason to build it than just to make things disappear."

"*Things* don't disappear, Betty. Only living flesh. Don't ask me why."

"I suppose you wonder where it goes?"

He nodded. "That's the reason for the big Needle." He explained about the little one, how they saw uses for it in surgery, in diagnosis, why nobody would risk one if he didn't know where his disappearing body part was going. "We built it big enough to go into so we could find out where the body member goes. But there have been two mistakes and we don't want a third." He watched the workmen for a while, saying nothing. Then, "I suppose I should have stayed in Florida. But then if I were there I'd be coming back now to find out what this is all about."

"What's in Florida?" Betty asked. She turned to him a little too brightly, he thought.

"A place called Pelican Rock. Bought it, but never had a chance to live in it until this winter. And then this Needle business came up. My wife and two kids are still down there. Ever been to Florida?"

"No. Frank and I think we'll do it some day. Either Florida or California. Don't know which. Just seems sensible to live in a place that demands less of your body."

"Are you working for that day? Is that why you took this job?"

"No," she said. "I have a boy, Jimmy. I've taken care of Jimmy for six years and now he's in school and I don't have anything to do—Oh, I don't want you to misunderstand me. I could find a million things around the house to do. But there's Frank's mother. She's staying with us and gives Jimmy his lunch. She knows I like to work, so we made a deal: She does all the housework and I come home with a pay check.

With both Frank and me working, we have a little left over these days."

"I know what you mean. I have two boys. They're a little older than Jimmy and they're costing a lot, too."

"You look tired."

"I *am* tired. I don't know when I've been so tired. I haven't been up all night since I was in college. We used to play bridge two days running. But I bet I couldn't go to sleep if I tried."

"Why don't you lean over this way?" Betty said. "Put your head on my lap and I'll massage your forehead. I had my night's sleep and I feel fine. I don't mind, really."

Her hands were cool and soft, as he knew they would be, and she had the good sense not to say anything while she moved her fingers over his hot forehead. He could not remember anything so pleasant and so relaxing and he was on the point of falling asleep when loud voices from the direction of the Needle made him sit up.

Several people he had not seen before were talking with the policeman stationed at the gate of the fence workmen were constructing. The officer was waving his arms around, pointing frequently to the entrance office and shaking his head. The three people, a large man, a small man and a woman, did not seem to understand.

"I've been watching them," Betty said. "They walked in when the policeman at the office left his post for a moment."

"I wonder who they are." Devan jumped down from the packing box, flexed his muscles, was satisfied to feel the rush of blood through his arms and legs. The near-nap had done him some good. "Where is everybody?"

Betty came off the crate, stood beside him. "There are only a few policemen left. And I don't see any newspaper people at all."

Devan glanced up at the windows of Dr. Costigan's office, saw Sam Otto's face in the window, his eyes looking over Devan's head at the three people at the Needle.

"I'd like to get out of here," Devan said.

"You want to go home?"

"No. I mean I'd like to breathe some fresh air for a change." He walked up the steps to the office door, Betty behind him. They went in.

Dr. Costigan was asleep at his desk, his head in his arms.

Orcutt glanced at them with sleepy eyes; he was leaning back comfortably in another chair.

"Tennis, anyone?" Devan asked.

"Go to hell," Sam Otto said from the window. "Not that I ever played tennis."

Orcutt rose and stretched. "Well, Dev, what's to become of the project now?"

"I haven't thought about that," Devan said. "I've been wondering what happens to us."

"We'll probably go to jail before it's all over," Tooksberry said. "I called my wife and she thinks I'm there already. Nearly hung up on me."

"We're going to have visitors," Sam said.

"Who?" Orcutt asked, not getting up. "I hope it's not for questions again."

"Some people who were arguing with the policeman at the Needle are coming this way."

A few minutes later the three who had slipped past the police guard at the door came into the room with a policeman.

"These three say they have a message from your boss," the officer said. "Do you know them?"

The three stood side by side near the door. The tall man had the weight to match, carried himself proudly nonetheless—perhaps a little too proudly, Devan thought. His chin was so high, in fact, he looked as if he were seeing everything through the crescent part of bifocals, yet he didn't wear glasses. The lip beneath a long cigar matched his chin; they were both massive. His eyes were fiery, his long, black overcoat was several seasons out of style and the belt was not tied. His black hat was battered but Devan had to admit it was clean.

There was a woman on his left, a bent-over woman with a hatchet nose, bulging eyes, black scraggly hair showing from beneath an old black hat. Her lips were pressed firmly together.

The man on the big man's right was as erect as a man could be, his feet forming a V, his shoulders back, his suit neatly pressed, from what Devan could see of it between the folds of the open topcoat. His face was nothing unusual, but there was a fanatical gleam in the eyes.

The three stood there, the big man looking them over one at a time, the woman staring disdainfully at Betty, the man simply at attention, eyes straight ahead.

"Never saw these people before in my life, Officer," Devan said.

"Neither have I," Orcutt said. The others nodded.

"Who's in charge here?" thundered the big man.

"What do you want?" Devan countered, angered by the loud voice and gruff manner.

"We have a message from The Boss," the man said.

"Who's that?" Sam Otto asked.

"Who else but God?" the large man said. "We are His children. I'm Eric Sudduth of the Sudduth Rescue Mission down the street here, Grand Director of the Rescue of the Willing and the Wise. This," he said, indicating the woman, "is Sister Abigail, Directress of the Labor of Women for Rescue and Redemption. This Eminent Brother is Orvid Blaine, Assistant Director of the Work."

Devan nodded. "I'm Devan Traylor." He introduced the others. "What do you want with us?"

"You must turn off the machine," Sudduth said. "God has told us you are interfering with His work and will. Two have been sacrificed to prove what happens when you violate The Boss's orders. The machine must be destroyed."

"Amen," Sister Abigail said.

"You better do like the man says," the Assistant Director said between his teeth. "We don't want to fool around with God's will."

"I'm sorry I brought these people in here," the policeman said. "I thought they knew you. This man here said—"

"Turn off the machine and there'll be glory for you and glory for me!" Sister Abigail's smile revealed a picket fence of teeth.

Devan caught Orcutt's eye, saw mirrored there the embarrassment he felt. There was a period of silence which became more unbearable the longer it stretched; it reminded Devan of an amateur play in which one of the participants had forgotten his line and the others were unable to go on because their lines had to be cued by the forgetful thespian.

"All right," the officer said, jumping into the breach. "Come on, you three. Out you go." He moved to step in front of them.

"Wait a minute," Devan said. "I'm sure these people are well-intentioned. They must feel very strongly about what they believe to barge in here this way."

"You'd better turn it off, mister," Blaine said menacingly. "You heard what the Grand Director said."

"I don't know about God's will, but I do know we have to keep the Needle going so the two men in the Eye can find their way back here."

"There is no way back," Sudduth said. "There is no turning back on what's been done."

"Just what is your racket?" Orcutt asked.

"You better watch that—"

"Quiet, Orvid." Eric Sudduth drew in his breath with dignity, glared at his questioner. "It is obvious to me, sir, that your intelligence has not allowed you that grander vision, that greater view of this troubled world that we have so that you could participate in the great work we are doing. The world is in its present crisis because of men like you and it is our allotted task to bring you into the fold."

"What's that got to do with the Needle?" Sam Otto asked.

"It has everything to do with it. The two men you so unceremoniously annihilated with the machine might some day have been led to the light."

"You mean they might have some day joined your Rescue Mission, is that it?" Devan said.

"We don't have the whole world to draw on," Sudduth said.

"We must be careful about what we allow to occur in this neighborhood. The forces of law and order may let you do what you will about letting people walk into annihilation, but as Grand Director of our Rescue Work, I cannot allow it. Especially so close to home."

Orcutt snorted. "You couldn't feel any worse about losing a couple potential converts than we do about losing the men themselves."

"We can't allow any more to go through. You must turn off the machine."

"Turn it off in the name of the Grand Director," Sister Abigail said. "Turn it off in the name of the master! In Glory's name!"

"That will suffice, Sister," Sudduth said.

"We can't turn it off," Devan said.

"This way!" The policeman suddenly came to life, opened the door.

"The Grand Director said turn it off," Blaine said, his eyes dark, his face set. He walked toward Devan.

"You, too," the policeman said, coming forward and catching Blaine by the arm.

Blaine broke away and the policeman caught his arm again, twisting it behind him, leading him to the doorway.

"It will go hard with all of you," Sudduth said before he went out.

"You can't disobey the master!" the woman screamed.

"Amen!" Blaine yelled.

The policeman pushed him out the door.

8

It was unfortunate that the Chicago Police Department was forced to admit there was such a thing as Costigan's Needle, especially since two persons had disappeared within it, and that this property of the device was easily demonstrable, for this very admission placed squarely on the shoulders of the department the responsibility of bringing back either or both of the vanished men. And this they could not do.

A cat in a tree is a neighborhood crisis with at least one last resort: the fire department can be called and the cat brought down by a fireman who simply crawls up a ladder to get it, though this practice is frowned upon but tolerated by every department across the land. Still, no more certain way of rescuing a cat has been found.

A murder has a routine procedure: Look for the murderer. Police departments, while not always finding the murderer, at least go through the motions of looking for him.

When a man disappears into a sixty-foot Needle and you don't know where the Eye of the Needle goes... Well, no precedent has yet been established here. What to do?

First, the police had tried to learn everything they could about the Needle. They took page after page of notes from all who were associated with the Needle in any capacity whatsoever and, with the exception of the actual secret of the construction of the Needle itself, Devan figured the police learned everything there was to know about it.

"What's the next step?" Lieutenant Johnson asked. "A guy can't walk into the Eye or he disappears. He can't hold onto anything like a rope because if he did he'd disappear and the rope he'd have been holding would still be here. How to go about trying to get Griffin and Basher back? It's got me whipped and I hate to admit it."

"Well," Devan said drily, feeling a lot of time had been wasted in note-taking, "one thing: You boys now know as much as we do."

While the police pondered and the public waited, the Needle current stayed on. Dr. Costigan arranged the circuits and dials so that any change in current or voltage level was immediately compensated for and nothing short of loss of power from outside would affect the Eye area.

Though many persons gave Glenn Basher and Detective Griffin up for dead, nobody mentioned it; everyone expressed the hope that now that the Needle was working twenty-four hours a day, the two might find the opening and come staggering back to the safety of this side of the Eye.

In the meantime, nearby traffic had to be detoured to other streets. The curious formed long lines of cars that went slowly by, faces at the car windows. Crowds were always walking by, hoping for a look at the Needle or the people involved. The police kept them moving.

The only persons allowed inside the building, besides the regular office force, the Inland executives, the police, the press and radio men, were a long string of specialized people, more than a score of names that would have made a glittering roster of the gifted, intelligent and learned. Physicists from universities and research centers in the Middle West, electronics experts from far and near, navy men, army men, doctors, radiologists, mathematicians, people from Great Lakes Naval Training Center, men from Rantoul where the big air force base was, research men from Cook County Hospital, Illinois Research, the Nelson Morris Institute of Medical Research, from the University of Illinois Medical School, from Los Alamos, Yucca Flat-Devan lost track of all who came by.

They gawked, they put their hands through the barrier and drew them back with a cry. They looked in amazement, they frowned, they sat down and stared. But not one of them could explain it or offer a suggestion about what to do next. They all wanted to talk about it, though. Some wanted to talk about how close they had come to inventing a thing like the Needle. Others wanted to discuss how amazing it was that it had not been invented before. Still others were only fishing for information that couldn't be supplied simply because the man who could have told them refused to see them. Dr. Costigan would not even talk with anyone from Claybourne, his alma mater, and Dewhurst, his most recent school. Others, after the first few interrogators, followed his example.

It was Sam Otto who came up with the idea three days later. It was the sight of a uniformed policeman drawing back one eager woman biologist (she wanted to put her arms into the Eye up to her elbows) that popped the thought into Sam's head.

At the time Devan was talking to Betty who, as Dr. Costigan's girl of all work, found herself with little to do now that the Needle was finished. They were chatting in the doctor's office, not paying any attention to Sam at the window.

"I've got it! I've got it!" Sam cried suddenly, turning away.

"Hey, look! Oh, you missed it! That big guard out there. He pulled that woman away from the Eye."

Devan and Betty stood up. They sat down again.

"So what?" Devan said.

"Don't you get it?" Sam asked excitedly.

"Whatever in the world are you talking about, Sam?" Betty asked.

"The guard that pulled the woman away," he said. He became exasperated. "Look: what do we want most?"

"To bring back Basher and Griffin," Devan said.

"Right. But we couldn't think of a way. But I just have." Sam smiled at them and seemed to get some satisfaction in withholding the information for a moment. "You can't tie a rope around a guy and let him wander into the Eye because the rope's not alive? Right?"

"Yes. For heaven's sake—"

"So, let's make a rope of human beings!" Sam said triumphantly. "Get it? We can join hands and somebody can step into the Eye and we've got hold of him and the second guy can step in and the third—there'll be enough making the string to let them go as far as we want. When they go in so far, those on this side can pull them out."

"I think he's got the answer," Betty said.

"I'll be damned," Devan said. "It's so simple, it's a wonder somebody hasn't already thought of it."

"Operation Otto" was to have been a simple affair with Dr. Costigan, Sam Otto, James Holcombe, Devan Traylor, Edmund Orcutt and Howard Tooksberry forming one end of the chain and volunteers who wanted to bring Glenn Basher and the detective back forming the other end. It was hoped enough policemen would volunteer to provide the necessary ballast.

But as soon as the police heard about it, they insisted on taking over and ruled that no Inland people were to enter the Eye. The boys in blue themselves would rescue Mr. Basher and Mr. Griffin, one of Chicago's finest. The commissioner ruled that volunteers would have to pass a rigid physical examination. They could have no prosthetic appliances anywhere in the body, no filled teeth (except for a few minor cavities for which arrangement for refilling could be made immediately after coming back out of the Eye) and they'd have to be single and under thirty years of age. The day was set for three days from then and the time was set for eight in the evening.

As soon as the newspapers and radio networks learned of the proposed project, "Operation Otto" became something of a sensation. Once again crowds swarmed the streets around the Rasmussen Stove Company and police had to rope off the area. Cars clogged the neighboring streets filled with the curious who, on the early spring evenings, had nothing better to do.

The time intervening allowed interviews with Dr. Costigan and others close to the Needle by radio, news and TV men who all wanted to know what the possibilities and probabilities in the case might be. Devan and the others got tired of saying they knew nothing that the public didn't already know, that anyone's guess was as good as theirs.

On the day of the experiment the fence around the Needle was removed. They learned why when they saw workmen erecting bleachers around the Needle at a considerable distance. Devan figured the platform with a low railing and draped with red, white and blue bunting would be a place for dignitaries.

"Wonder if we're going to be allowed to witness it?" Devan said sarcastically when he called Orcutt at the Inland plant to tell him what was happening. Orcutt had been spending most of his time in the recent days catching up with his work at the big plant.

"I got a ticket in the mail," Orcutt said. "There's one down here for you, too. It says 'Operation Otto' is scheduled for tonight. It further states the big doors are to close at a quarter to eight."

"No R.S.V.P.?"

Orcutt laughed. "They know damn well nobody'll miss it."

"Who's putting out the tickets, do you suppose?"

"Mayor's office."

At sundown, spotlights which had been put up outside in the area around the building were turned on. They gave the event the flavor of a Hollywood movie premiere.

The lights were bright because TV and newsreel cameras were to be used everywhere.

Policemen in great numbers gathered about the vicinity of the building and several in special uniforms at the door examined the tickets of all who entered. The guests strode down the corridors on either side to the rear where they turned toward the center and came into the big room through the open door in the center. At seven-thirty the room was stuffy with smoke and alive with the roar of conversation.

At exactly twenty minutes before the hour, four police cars drew up before the building, bringing twelve spotlessly attired policemen who fell into formation when they got out of the cars and marched through the doors of the building two abreast.

Theirs was the place of honor in the reserved area before the Needle's Eye, all of them clear-eyed, ramrod straight, jut-jawed and stern. They were obviously the city's best and Devan wondered how many filled teeth they had among them.

The police brass, the city politicos and dignitaries all took their seats in the reserved area to the right of the Needle's Eye. Devan counted five hundred people in various sections of the room, wondered who and what at least four hundred of them were.

Devan and the members of the board of directors of Inland Electronics and those connected officially with the Needle sat in a small roped-off section to the right of the volunteer policemen. Orcutt, Holcombe and Tooksberry were more or less indifferent to what was going on because they had been part of it before and now could only stand by and observe what the city had turned the Needle into, but other members of the board were not silent and unmoved by the circus atmosphere. Mrs. Petrie had forsaken her knitting and sat open-mouthed for the most part; Homer Parrett stared at the Eye, the bigwigs and the volunteers in turn while he chewed his cigar; Clarence Gleckman champed his gum with unconscious savagery; and Spencer O'Grady looked uncomfortable and a little fearful, not knowing what to expect.

Precisely at eight o'clock the mayor mounted the little platform to the right of the Needle's Eye. He addressed himself to the twelve volunteers. He told them of the honor they were doing Detective Griffin and Mr. Basher, and underscored their bravery. He touched on their patriotism, on the efficiency of the city administration and its various departments. He then commented on the Needle itself, praising it as a product of free enterprise. When he concluded his talk, he bowed first to the applause, then in the direction of the television cameras because that is where there were more eyes and ears.

The last thing the mayor did before moving from the speaker's stand was to introduce Lieutenant Johnson, who in turn introduced a sergeant named Spencer who reminded Devan of an infantry physical-training instructor he had known. Sergeant Spencer bawled instructions at the twelve volunteers.

The policemen were stripping. They took off everything except briefs, tennis shoes and socks, then each took a turn at a resin bag.

It was a breathless moment when they all joined hands and the sergeant yelled more orders. They walked, a wonderful display of muscles and coordination, all of them young and agile, toward the Eye, each holding the hand of the man behind him, with the exception of the first man who had the resin bag in his right hand. They stopped.

As they stood at the Eye's opening, they threw the resin bag around among themselves until all were satisfied. Then they threw the bag to the sergeant. He barked an order and they all got in chain formation again.

The first man walked bravely into the Eye, chin up, chest out.

Instantly the second man gave a cry and went down to his knees, his right arm, muscles powerfully knotted, extending down into the Eye. He was gritting his teeth. Those behind him were tense, were pulling away from the Needle.

"I'll go in," the policeman rasped. "I've still got him, but he's *down*."

The line eased him into the Eye.

The third policeman, his body wet with sweat that reflected the lights brightly from bunched muscles, now went through the agony at the Eye's opening. He could say nothing, he was straining so hard. Little by little his feet were sliding toward the opening and he and everyone else watched the progress of his feet inch by inch across the floor.

The nine other policemen had no difficulty in holding the line, but the third policeman nodded toward the Eye and his buddies moved forward with him until he slipped over the edge little by little.

When the third policeman disappeared, the fourth policeman fell flat on the floor, his right arm disappearing into the Eye at floor level. His eyes were bright and round, the white showing more than it should have, his tongue between his teeth, and his face at first red, then a darker red, and finally purple.

Suddenly he gasped and collapsed, his head, which he had managed to hold off the floor a few inches, hitting the floor with a dull thud as the pull of his eight colleagues yanked him away from the Needle's Eye.

His right hand was empty.

There was a gasp from many throats, then there was a silence so quiet it hurt Devan's ears. Then all that could be heard was the weeping of a man who had to let go.

9

"It was horrible," Miss Treat said. "I saw it on TV."

"You and a few million more," Devan said, hanging his coat in his office closet and wishing Miss Treat, who had followed him in, would go away. "Last night is one night I want to forget." He meant that in more ways than one. Devan eased himself gently into his desk chair; any sudden, violent motion, he knew, would snap his head off his shoulders.

"You look ill." Miss Treat, he knew, was examining him closely. Mustn't give any sign, I suppose. "Are you sick, Mr. Traylor?" He would have laughed if he had had the energy. He couldn't say he was ill because then she'd be too solicitous.

"Yes and no," he said, finally. "Yes, if illness is how you feel, no if you mean the bug-inspired kind of sickness. To be quite frank with you, Miss Treat, my indisposition comes from something I drank. Do I make myself clear?"

"I think so," she said. He recalled that she had never seen him with a head like this before. "Can I get you some coffee?"

"That's an inspiration," he said. It sounded as if he meant it, but he actually wanted to be alone more than he wanted coffee. Even her voice was beginning to get on his nerves. "You needn't hurry back."

Miss Treat left him and when she closed the office door, everything closed in on him. He should have known better the night before, but the situation had demanded it and now, he knew, he'd have to pay. When you drink last night you borrow today's good feelings. It was an axiom. And then when you live today, all of today's good feelings you find were withdrawn from the bank of good feeling yesterday and aren't there. He tried massaging his temples. Sometimes that helped push the two parts of his head back together.

He could try to justify what he'd done. Three policemen had gone through the Eye the night before and weren't coming back. They had gone into the Eye under circumstances that he would never have allowed. All that show and pomp and then the miserable failure! The city and the police department should have turned the experiment over to Inland. Still, he couldn't say just *how* he'd have done it differently, but he was sure the fewer people there were around to observe it, the less hectic it would have been. The athletic policemen were pushed into the Eye because of the mayor's speech and the pressure of the onlookers much as a football player makes a tremendous run because of the thousands who yell hurrahs.

All that fanfare and show—and then, afterwards, the stunned silence, the waiting. Then the people who had so suddenly become very quiet left their seats and found their way out of the building, carrying with them the mental picture of three men who had stepped through the Needle's Eye that night, presumably never to return. Why should they return? Basher and Griffin had never come back.

He was one of the last to leave, still in a state of shock. He knew he couldn't sleep, couldn't eat, had a gnawing and undefined uneasiness. He went into the first tavern he could find.

Much later he went to his hotel in the Loop, had a few more drinks at the hotel bar and remembered becoming unnerved again when all the people at the bar could talk about was the three policemen who had gone through the Needle's Eye.

"You think that's on the level?"

"Naw, it's all done with mirrors."

"It's a big build-up for something. It'll end up being a big commercial."

"You don't believe in the Needle?"

"Listen, do you know anybody who ever saw it?"

"I never thought about that."

"They can do anything with trick photography."

"Anybody who thinks those people are disappearing is just plain nuts."

"Fill 'em up all the way around again, Ray."

"Yeah, give that glum-looking guy down at the end of the bar a drink, too. Looks like he could stand it."

"What's troubling you, buddy?"

That decided him. He bought a bottle and went to his room. In a little while he forgot all about Needles and Eyes and everything else, though now he vaguely remembered calling his wife later — much later. He was startled to recall that he had bawled like a baby through part of the call.

Sherman was only half right. War and the Day After were both hell. He massaged his temples again. He had tried running away from the problem and had succeeded, for a while. Now he had to think about the yawning Needle's Eye again.

Five guys walk through a Needle's Eye. A big Needle. With a big Eye. The last three trying to get the first two. And now all five of them are in there.

What would happen if I walked in? Say... he smiled to himself. Maybe everybody has the wrong idea. Maybe it's paradise on the other side of the Needle. And none of the men *want* to come back. Had anybody thought of that? But then he remembered how cold his arm got when he had put it in the hole of the first Needle. He decided paradise would never get that cold.

How to get five guys back — if they're still alive. But we've tried everything. Holding hands... Maybe we could get a snake long enough for a guy to hold onto and he could crawl into the Eye with it, somebody else holding the tail on this side of the Needle. It would have to be something like a snake. Something alive and long enough.

The jangling telephone roused him from his thoughts with a start. He answered it. It was Orcutt.

"Dev?"

"Yeah."

"This is Ed. Dev, for heaven's sake, where have you been? Where did you go last night? I thought maybe you'd gone back to Florida."

"Nearly did, Ed. I guess the fact that people go in and never come out has me down."

"I know just how you feel. I'll never forget that one policeman sobbing. That was awful."

"I had to get away from the Needle, Ed. I had to think of something else for a while."

"Everybody else, too."

"Anything interesting going on?"

"No. Nobody's being charged with anything and the city's putting the thing right back into our hands. They're giving us a clean slate and telling us to get to work bringing those guys back."

Devan laughed feebly. "Yeah. That's easy to do. We build a big thing like a Needle and then we don't know how to use it."

"Oh, we'll find a way, yet."

"I've heard that before. 'Operation Otto.'"

"The newspapers aren't indicting anybody, Dev. Editorials blame the police department more than they do us. They say the Needle is a purely scientific curiosity and that the police had no business fooling around with it."

"What's the public reaction?"

"We've had a million calls this morning. Half the people say turn the Needle off, destroy it and all the plans for it. The other half say leave the Needle turned on and encourage us to work to find a solution and bring the men back."

"The Needle still on?"

"I've left orders to leave it on, Dev. The city's still giving us police protection. We're going to need it, too. But from now on we're going back to private investigation. No peanuts and Cracker Jack this next time."

"If there is a next time," Devan said.

"There will be. Say, what the hell is wrong with you? I've never heard you so dejected. You'd better come on up to the office. You need cheering up."

"I will, later."

"Why later?"

"I've got a lot of thinking to do right now." He hung up, leaned back in his chair again.

Well, it was nice of the city not to blame anyone. If he had had his way, though, he and Orcutt, Dr. Costigan and the others would probably be where the policemen were. They'd have been on the disappearing end of the human chain. At least then he'd know what the other side of the Eye looked like....

Miss Treat came in smiling, Devan thought, a little too ingratiatingly. She put the cup and saucer on his desk. The coffee smelled good.

"Half a teaspoon of sugar and light on the cream."

"You've done it just right, Miss Treat."

"I remembered..."

He sipped the coffee and looked at her, regretfully realizing how little it would take to make it a matter of moonlight and roses and... There was something on her mind.

"You say you don't want to be reminded about last night," she said.

"Did I? Do you want to say something about it?"

"Yes." She colored faintly. "You want to get the men out, don't you?"

"Of course."

"Well..." She seemed embarrassed.

"Go on, Miss Treat. Do you have any ideas?"

"This is sort of silly," she said. "I'm sure somebody's thought of it. At least you can tell me why it won't work."

"Go ahead." He didn't expect much, but he was desperate enough to listen to anything.

She cleared her throat. "Well, Mr. Traylor, did you ever play Twenty Questions?"

"Of course." What was she driving at?

"Things are divided into three classes, aren't they?"

"Yes. Animal, vegetable and mineral."

"Don't you see what I mean?" she said eagerly. "There could be two divisions—animate and inanimate, really. But in Twenty Questions you tell which class it is, subdividing the animate."

A great light was turned on in Devan's mind. The warmth of its glow spread through his tired body, traveling down every nerve channel and relaxing him.

"Both animal *and* vegetable matter are alive," she said triumphantly.

Devan reached for the phone, dialed a number. He hoped Betty Peredge had reported for work. "You've done it, Miss Treat—maybe, that is. I don't want to say anything to anyone until I have the answer. We'll have to see about it first. Like Sam's idea, it may seem as if it's a solution and... Hello, Betty? Listen, Betty, have you plants in the windows there yet? Yes.... But you still have the sansevieria?... Good. Here's what I want you to do. Put it on a long board and shove it into the Needle, draw it out and tell me what happens. Call me back.... Yes, that's right. If it works we have Miss Beatrice Treat to thank. She's my secretary and she's standing right here right now.... Yeah. Call me back, will you? Right away."

A few minutes later the phone rang.

"Devan?"

"Yes."

"Betty."

"Yes, I know. Well...?"

"The flowerpot comes out but the flowers stay in."

When Betty Peredge proved that animal matter was not the only living substance that would go through the Eye, Devan did not shout for joy, remembering the madness that resulted from Sam Otto's suggestion, which, intelligently handled, might have proved to be of value but which could not be tried again.

Devan asked her first whether or not anyone had observed her little experiment. She said the policeman on duty inside the reinstalled fence had watched her closely but that she was sure he didn't see *exactly* what she had done.

"Let's assume he doesn't know what happened, then," Devan said. "And then let's keep quiet about it."

So Betty put down the phone and stared at her flowerless flowerpot while Devan and Miss Treat walked up to Orcutt's office.

"My God!" Orcutt said, his hand on the phone ready to lift it and call. "Let's get right on it! Now we know how to get those boys back!"

Devan put out a restraining hand. "That's not the way, Ed. We don't want a fiasco like last night with TV cameras, tickets and speeches, do we?"

Orcutt frowned. "I see what you mean."

By midafternoon a dozen workmen hired at triple pay dug up a Lombardy poplar tree twenty-five feet high from a back yard not six blocks from the factory site. The owner of the tree had been offered a price he could not turn down, no questions asked. He thought Devan was out of his mind but he was true to his word: he didn't ask one question.

The tree was laid on a large flat-bottomed truck trailer and moved slowly through city streets to the Rasmussen Stove Company where its entry into the inner building through the large rear door went without mishap. The tree's roots were enclosed in their original dirt in a hurriedly constructed wooden pot seven feet on the sides and eight feet deep; Devan didn't want to chance the tree's dying on the job.

"If it were any other kind of tree we'd have to cut off the branches to get it into the Eye and it might die," Devan explained as workmen moved it on dollies across the floor.

"When are you going to move it into the opening?" Betty asked.

"As soon as we get the group together. Has anybody come around today?"

"Everybody's been avoiding this place."

The news, of course, could not keep. It wasn't long before newsmen demanded entrance, according to the plant guard in the outside office. Devan went out to talk to them. A dozen men stood there.

"What's going on?" one of them asked. "Why can't we get in?"

"Yeah. Last night we were all over the place. What's up?"

"Somebody said you've got a tree in there."

"What are you going to do with it?"

Devan looked around at the alert faces, some of them familiar to him by this time, smiled and put his hands up for quiet. "I wondered how long it would be before you boys showed up," he said. "I don't suppose it would do any good to deny anything."

"What's the tree for?" Pencils poised.

"We're going to put it in the Eye." Pencils moved.

"Thought only living matter could go in."

"This is a living tree."

"But why put a tree in? It can't report back."

"Somebody can crawl out on the tree and back again," Devan explained.

"When's this going to take place?"

Devan shrugged. "We're trying to round up a few Inland people right now."

"When are *we* getting in?"

"When we get ready."

The newsmen and photographers protested, wanted to go in at once, so Devan, though he explained it might be hours before the trial, okayed their entrance, leaving it to the office guard to check their credentials.

Devan arranged for them to have one of the unused offices; there were phones there and the office window gave them a good view of the floor so they could tell when things were happening.

A little later Orcutt showed up. "Say, that's some tree you got." He moved along it, bent several of the branches and they snapped back into place. "Must be alive. Won't die in the warmth in here, will it?"

Devan shrugged. "I don't think it will. If it does, it won't be right away. There'll be plenty of time for experimenting."

"Let's wheel it to the Eye and see if it goes in."

A few minutes later Tooksberry and Holcombe came in and the four of them struggled beneath the many ceiling lights to push the tree that now lay across the three dollies.

"Somebody should have oiled the dolly wheels," Orcutt said between grunts, a shoulder against one of the smooth, bare branches.

"I thought poplar was a light wood," Devan said. "This one weighs a ton."

"It's that big pot," Orcutt said, jerking his thumb toward the root end.

Several newsmen who were watching the tree's progress across the floor came out of the office and helped push it toward the Eye. The tree rolled up to the fence, the men moved the fence open and then pushed the tree inch by inch inside the enclosure. Betty assisted by telling them which way to guide the treetop.

"You're right there," she announced finally. "A little more and it will be going in."

The crew pushed with renewed vigor and the dolly wheels protested in shrill screeches.

"It's in!"

They rushed to the front and saw that the top of the tree had vanished where it entered the energized area.

"It works," Orcutt said.

"Well," Devan said. "Let's push it halfway in, while we're at it."

"Might as well." Orcutt was wheezing from exertion. "But let's catch our breaths first." He sat on a nearby chair. "I've notified the board. They ought to be here. We sure could use them on this pushing detail, though."

"It *is* work," Holcombe said, sitting in another chair, mopping his forehead with a handkerchief.

"Who's going in this time?" Tooksberry asked.

"You volunteering?"

"Not me. You'll never get me in there."

Betty walked over to where Devan was standing beside the tree, felt of a branch and said in a whisper, "How many newsmen did you say there were? Twelve, wasn't it?"

"I think so." He thought a moment. "Yes. I'm sure that's right. Why?"

"Well, they're all out of the office—I went there to make sure—and I count only eleven. The five who helped are standing over there and six others are sitting in chairs. You count them."

He counted only eleven, too. "Check with the guard in the outer office, Betty. I could be wrong about that number."

"I called Lieutenant Johnson," Orcutt was saying. "Surprised he hasn't come in yet." He looked at his watch. "It's after five."

"Maybe he doesn't want to get in any deeper," Holcombe said.

"Who's going in it?" Tooksberry asked again.

"Somebody'd think you were worried about that, Howard," Orcutt said. "Why do you keep asking?"

Tooksberry's face showed his embarrassment. "Well, it's just something you haven't thought of. Who'd be silly enough to want to go now that everybody knows you don't come back?"

"That's why we have the tree," Devan explained patiently. "The tree disappears inside just as a human being does."

"You, maybe. Not me."

"Whoever goes in this next time can go in on the tree, just move along it and, after he's been inside long enough, move on out and report."

"Look who's coming," Holcombe said, looking toward the outer office door.

Dr. Costigan and Sam Otto slowly and erratically were moving across the floor, their arms about each other's waists. When they got close, the effects of their drinking were visible in their faces and in their eyes.

"What's goin' on?" Sam asked in a thick voice.

"Yeah. What'sha matter?"

Sam pointed to the doctor, said in an aside, "He always talks kinda funny when he's had a few."

The doctor stared straight ahead of him, his eyes steady, but because of a motion that began somewhere down by his ankles, his head had an erratic circular motion.

"We've been gone long time, Sham. A treesh growing outa the Eye."

Sam focused his eyes as best he could. "There *is* a tree there. Remarkable." He turned to Devan. "When did it start to grow?" He hiccupped, his unlighted cigar falling out of his mouth. He stooped, finally managed to pick it up.

"You fellows better go to the doctor's office," Orcutt said.

"You're a total loss as you are. Mrs. Peredge will order you some coffee."

"C'mon, Doc. Le's go see Mrs. Peredge."

"Yesh." The doctor would have bowed but Sam yanked his arm, pulled him away.

A few minutes later half the poplar tree went into the Eye. The tree's tight branches made it possible to move it into the four-foot opening without trimming a single one, as Devan knew it would. Looking at it from the side, it was as if someone had chopped the tree neatly off at the halfway mark. Those who had been pushing stood back to observe it.

"Well?" It was Tooksberry again.

"Yeah, I know," Orcutt said. "Who's going in it? Frankly, I don't know. I'd like to."

"Uh-huh," Devan said. "I've got as much right as you."

"Look," Orcutt said, turning to him. "We're not going to argue again, are we?"

"I hope not."

"Your problem is solved." A young man who had been standing near by came over to them. "I'm Jed Huston of the *Sun-Times*. I'd like to go."

"You're crazy," Tooksberry said. "Don't you know nobody's come back?"

Jed, a medium-sized, crop-eared man in a neat plaid suit, flashed him a smile. "I know what it's all about; I've kept up with it. It would be dangerous just to walk in. But now that you have a tree to climb in on, how could a guy lose? You climb in and climb out just as if the tree was out over a riverbank."

"Yes," Tooksberry said gravely, "but being out on a limb can be a dangerous thing."

"I'm willing to take the chance. I'd bring back quite a story if I succeeded. What do you say?" He smiled again. There was a lot of humor in his blue eyes and, though he was slight of build, there was a certain sureness and smoothness about his actions that spoke well for his muscular fitness.

It was after six o'clock when the matter was finally settled. As soon as the other newspapermen heard Huston had volunteered to climb into the Eye on the tree, they all wanted to do it. But since Huston had been the first to volunteer, he was given the job.

By the time Jed Huston was ready to climb on the tree and edge his way into the Eye, all the board members, Lieutenant Johnson, and Miss Treat had answered Orcutt's invitation by appearing for the test.

"We thought it might prove an impossible task, this trying to find a way to rescue the men in the Eye," Orcutt explained to everyone. "But Miss Beatrice Treat, whom I'm sure many of you know as Mr. Traylor's secretary, came to our rescue with a simple solution. It takes an alert mind to think out a difficult problem so that the result seems quite simple and everybody can do it after that." There was applause from the small group and Orcutt explained further what Miss Treat's idea was and how the experiment was to be conducted.

Then Orcutt introduced Jed Huston, who had disrobed to his underwear. He would have worn nothing, since he knew he was going to lose his clothes in the Eye anyway, but he wore his shirt and shorts in deference to Miss Treat, Mrs. Peredge and Mrs. Petrie.

He flashed them all a smile, then jumped athletically from the floor, catching hold of several branches and swinging himself to the top of the lengthwise tree.

He started to work his way cautiously toward the Eye.

"Wait!"

The yell came from another part of the room and heads swiveled on necks trying to locate the owner of the voice.

"Don't go in!"

Eyes came to focus on the far wall where, atop one of the large instrument panels, stood a man, his arms held high to draw attention. He was too far away to identify.

"No one is to go into the Needle's Eye, brethren."

Devan knew who it was then.

"The Grand Director of the Rescue of the Willing and the Wise has spoken," Orvid Blaine said. "Even now Director Sudduth, Sister Abigail and twenty-two Workers for Rescue and Redemption are praying for you who have led five to their deaths in violation of God's will."

Jed Huston had stopped to stare at the man. Now he started toward the Eye again.

"Stop, I say!" The man bent down, picked up a long, iron pipe. "One step farther and I'll throw this pipe down into all these wires. That will stop you."

Huston stopped then and sat on a branch, elbow on knee, chin on fist.

"I forgot to tell you," Betty whispered to Devan. "There were *twelve* newspapermen. I couldn't get the information to you because I had to get some coffee for the doctor and Sam Otto."

Devan remembered the familiar face. "I should have known. I looked straight at him, too."

Orcutt was on his feet. "Listen, Blaine," he said. "We realize you feel you're doing right and we won't say anything if you just get down quietly and leave the building."

"Otherwise," Lieutenant Johnson said, "you'll end up in the pokey and I'll take pleasure in arranging it myself."

"Blaine," Devan said, getting up and joining Johnson and Orcutt halfway across the floor. "If you let that pipe drop to those wires, you will be the cause of the death of five men because you will be cutting off their escape from the other side of the Needle's Eye. They won't have a way to get back if you put this Needle out of commission."

"Just tell that man not to go into the Eye, that's all," Blaine said. "Nobody more is supposed to go in there now."

"That's enough," Johnson said. "You've shot off your mouth enough, I think. Now just jump down and we'll see that you get escorted to the door. You're interrupting an important experiment."

"I'm warning you," Blaine said, holding the pipe high in the air. "This goes in the wires if you don't tell the man to get down off the tree."

"Blaine, I'm giving you your last chance. Either jump down right now or I'm coming up to get you."

Blaine stood uncertain, his eyes big, his tongue running over his lips.

"We'll put you away for a long time," Orcutt said. "You'd better do what the lieutenant says. That wiring is worth a lot of money."

Lieutenant Johnson started for the panel, taking a nearby chair with him.

"I'm coming up, Blaine. No funny stuff or you'll be sorry."

"You stay back!" The man backed away, his mouth working, his face white.

Suddenly, when Johnson was on the chair ready to boost himself to the top of the panel, Blaine yelled in a strident voice, "I told you!"

Then he hurled the pipe downward with force.

A shower of sparks flew up from the panel.

Costigan's Needle shuddered. At eight spots on the hull of the Needle appeared dull red, then bright red, then brilliant orange circles. Metal buckled and the lights went out.

A few minutes later, when the metal cooled, it made crackling noises. As the metal contracted, it turned the tip a little to one side.

The room was full of smoke.

There was no sound. Nothing stirred.

Everything living within a two-block radius of Costigan's Needle had vanished. Bacteria, human beings, lice, alley cats, yeast, goldfish, grass—all these living things had gone where the five people had gone earlier: through the Eye. Only this time it was an incredibly enlarged Eye, a greatly magnified Eye because of an unprecedented and accidental surge of high-voltage electricity through certain of its solenoids.

The things that remained behind were in little piles here and there wherever there had been people: dental fillings, bridge-work, dentures, glasses, glass eyes, wigs, false eyelashes, trusses, artificial accessories that had been obvious, others that had been hidden. Now they all lay in plain sight for everyone to see, from the neat rows of clothing of those persons who had been kneeling in prayer at Sudduth's Rescue Mission to the paw prints of three dogs that had been engaged in a struggle in an alley a block away from the Needle.

Cars that had been whizzing down the affected streets went on without drivers and crashed. All that remained inside the cars were piles of clothing where the drivers and passengers had been sitting.

In all, three hundred and ninety-five persons had made the transition.

Part Two: Displacement

10

The lights went out and his chair was pulled from beneath him. It was purely a reflex action, the gasp that Devan gave, but it served him well because before he expelled the breath he was surrounded by water. This was unexpected and frightening and he thrashed about wildly. The more he struggled, the more he needed new air and the more need there was for him to reach the surface, so he increased his efforts and still he did not emerge....

Reason took over and he stopped working his arms and legs so frantically. Though the water was heavy against his eardrums and his lungs ached for air, he forced himself to remain calm. In a moment his face popped into cold air and he breathed huge chunks of wonderful air.

After several gulps of fresh air he became aware of the commotion around him, the churning and splashing of many people, occasional bits of water spattering his face, the cries of men and women, the gurgling sounds as people went under. He kicked himself as high out of the water as he could, saw faintly a dark clump of something that looked as if it might be land to his left, started to swim toward it.

A hand grasped his shoulder, fingernails cutting in deep. An arm circled his neck and threatened to cut off his air. He could hear hoarse breathing in his ear. With this added weight he sank beneath the waves, hearing a confusion of sounds as he went down. His assailant did not move but clung tighter instead.

Using both hands and summoning all his strength, Devan pried the arm away from around his neck. He kicked for the surface just as the other arm went around his neck and the body moved to face him. They shot through the surface, gasping for breath. In the dim light of night as they bobbed on the water he could see the woman's terrified, wild-eyed face. It belonged to Betty Peredge. She was looking through him.

He slapped her hard. Recognition came into her eyes.

"Let go, Betty!"

"I—I can't!" she sobbed, struggling closer, clinging frantically to him. They went under again. This time he pushed violently upward and as they emerged he struck at her head with his fist.

She let go for a moment, would have grabbed him again if he hadn't got hold of her long hair, held her away, her head dipping in and out of the water, her nails making shreds of the skin of his arm.

"Stop it!" he yelled.

Betty hung onto his arm, taking deep breaths and coughing.

"I'll take you to shore," he said. "Relax."

He came up behind her and she did not resist. He cupped one hand under her chin and towed her on her back. She grabbed his hand occasionally, then remembered and let go. In a matter of moments they were making progress in one direction, but Devan was at a disadvantage because he could not lift himself out of the water to see where he was going. He thought he heard waves lapping at a shore to his left, once saw a dog paddle by bound that way, but he could not rely on his hearing because of the shouting and splashing that was still going on around them. Trusting the dog and what he hoped were his own unerring senses, he turned toward his left and struck off that way.

Arm, exhale, legs, inhale. Reach, arm. Exhale. Scissor, legs. Inhale. Stretch, arm. Exhale. Work, legs. Inhale. Over and over, got to get to shore wherever that is, this way, don't give up. God, don't let me give up! Arm, exhale, legs, inhale, pull, exhale, push, inhale, over and over. Soon he became oblivious to the cold of the water and the feel that he was doing anything at all. It was like a dream. Arm, exhale, legs, inhale.

How much later was it when his arm touched bottom, when his feet brushed bottom, smooth sand, welcome sand? He did not know. He pulled Betty by him until her head struck sand and then she rolled slowly over on her stomach, dug hands into the mushy sand, tried to move farther inshore, could not, lay there moaning. Then she was sick.

Devan was too weak to do anything but watch through eyes that distorted and blurred and he wondered momentarily where he was and who this person near him was. He then became suddenly comfortable, tired and lazy. It was so pleasant, really, lying there, and he was going to sleep, he so needed sleep, beautiful sleep...

No. He must not go to sleep. He forced himself up the shore, stood up, leaned over and pulled Betty up the beach a little.

With a shock he saw that she was naked. Then he realized he was, too.

The shock passed as quickly as it had come in the moonlight on the beach. A warm breeze—it seemed warm after the cold water—brushed them dry in a few moments and they revived somewhat, sitting together on the sand, their breaths no longer labored.

They still had no energy for talk. They looked around, saw that there were others on the beach, some lying on the sand, others sitting and several standing, from what they could make out in the moonlight. There was no sound except the faint whisper of the waves on the shore.

"What happened?" Betty whispered.

Devan grunted. "I wish I knew."

They stood up, unsteady on their feet. Betty put her arm around him for support and he put his arm around her waist and they managed to walk slowly down the beach, seeing that others were coming in on the waves, hugging the sand when they reached shore. One man was giving artificial respiration to another. Several persons lay face down in the waves, bobbing gently there.

"Help, mister!" Devan felt someone grab his arm. "Help me, please! It's Ma. We think she's dead." He looked around. It was a boy of about ten years of age standing there looking frightened and dismayed, pulling his arm.

They followed the lad, walking among people groaning, moaning, sleeping or lying dazed on the beach. Finally they came to two children who were sobbing over an inert form on the cold sand.

Devan remembered he had seen a new method of artificial respiration but could not recall the details of it. He decided to waste no time trying to figure it out, put the woman's head on her hands in the old system, used his finger to draw the tongue out of her throat, then knelt and pressed the small of her back, releasing her, lifting her pelvis from the ground.... He knew from the beginning the woman and mother was probably dead. She was like ice.

"I'll spell you when," Betty said, standing beside the boy in the moonlight, her arms around his shoulders, her body perfectly silhouetted in the moonlight.

"I'll let you know." As he worked he looked at the two children, girls, who had stopped their sobbing, their eyes as big as saucers, watching, hoping for the first sign of life from their mother. Devan didn't have the heart to quit, to tell them what he thought. He'd keep on until his arms fell off.

Press and lift, press and lift. As he kept on he noticed a man sitting near by who was watching him in fascination, glancing now and then at Betty. Devan didn't like the expression on the half face the moonlight presented. There was another man not ten feet behind him who had become aware of what was going on around him, too.

Press and lift, press and lift. The man who had been watching rose to his feet, turned to them and walked slowly over. When he was within a few feet of Betty he swerved, grabbed the arm she had around the boy's shoulders and pulled her toward him.

Devan had no alternative. He reached the struggling couple at the same time as the second man. The second man reached out, yanked the first man's head back by the hair, hit him in the face. The man dropped.

"Thanks," Devan said to the man standing over the fallen one. "Thanks a lot." He came up to see what manner of man it was who lay on the sand, never saw the fist coming. It smashed into his face with sledge-hammer force and he felt the beach hit his back.

If it had not been for the fact that the hurtling body momentarily blocked out the moon, giving Devan warning of its coming, he might have been seriously hurt. The man was a fighter, no doubt of that. Devan rolled quickly to one side, jumped to his feet, turned in time to see a face beautifully unprotected as the man, surprised, started to his feet.

It was easier hitting the face than he thought it would be. And once the lead was on Devan's side, it was not too difficult following it up with similar devastating punches.

When it was over, Devan's knuckles were bleeding.

"Let's get out of here," he said.

"What about the woman?"

"Come on," Devan said, guiding her across the beach. "We've just discovered this isn't Main and Elm Streets. There are no police to call."

They walked unmolested across the sand which soon gave way to dry grass. The old grass was taller the farther they walked into it, ankle high at first, then knee high and almost waist high before they came to a grove of trees. They stopped. The only sound was the gentle soughing of the warm breeze through bare branches and bushes.

Betty shivered.

"Cold?"

She nodded.

"Lie down."

She looked at him with concern for a moment.

"I'll cover you with enough grass to keep you warm."

"What about you?"

"I'll manage."

She came over to him, her dark eyes frightened, her jet-black hair blowing first on the front side of her shoulder above her breast and then up and over her shoulder again. She pressed his arm with her hands. "Don't leave me," she said.

"I won't. I'll be near by."

"I—I want you next to me," she said. "I'd be afraid if I couldn't touch you, if I didn't know you were there, Devan."

Later, as they lay together, warmed by each other beneath a great heap of dry grass they had gathered, Devan envied Betty her sleep, though it gave him pleasure to think she trusted him enough, that she felt safe enough to sleep. She was exhausted and so was he. Her eyes closed almost at once when she lay down but he knew there could be no sleep for him because of what he had seen on the beach. The men there would soon come to life, if they had not already, and would wander about and... well, he wouldn't be surprised again.

To keep himself awake and still not move and disturb Betty and the blanket of grass, Devan kept every sense alert, listening for any sound above the distant murmur of the surf, the crackle of stepped-on grass or twigs, the sound of voices, the thud of footsteps on the earth.

Where was this? From where he lay he could look over the smooth curve of Betty's shoulder through a tangle of crosshatch grass to see stars. He had seen a moon before, too. It must be Earth, he reasoned. Where else could it be?

It was obvious many people had, through some electrical fluke, gone through the Needle's Eye, their transmigration a direct result of Blaine's dropping a pipe into the wiring system behind the panel. That much was pretty plain.

But if they had, then they had followed four policemen and Glenn Basher. Wasn't that true? Well, where were Basher and Griffin, then? Perhaps they had not survived the fall into the water. But they were men, all young. If any could have made it, they should have.

Was the Needle a time machine? When you dropped through the Eye, did you go back a thousand years or forward a thousand years? If it was a time machine, then what period of history was this? Certainly it could not be forward, otherwise there would be buildings and people—he hoped there would be people. Surely everybody didn't get wiped out with the H-bomb.

He brought his thoughts back into focus. Who were the people he had seen on the beach? How far had the area of the Needle's influence carried? He had seen perhaps two hundred people all together. Where had they all come from? Had Dr. Costigan made it? Had the others who had been with him near the Needle come through?

He snorted at the impossibility of answering these last questions while lying where he was and Betty moved a little in her sleep. He was quiet again.

Where is this? What year is it? To answer that, of course, would mean he was assuming the Needle was a time machine and he felt loath to make that assumption simply because it was so fantastic. Yet what else was there to assume? He and others had dropped through the Needle's Eye. They dropped through because where they were now was thousands of years before Chicago and the White Man and—but what about the Ice Age? No, the glaciers had built the ground up to the level of the Needle's Eye and where they were now was before the glaciers came down from the north.

Or was it? He was getting mixed up. Were the Great Lakes made by glaciers? Then this lake was really Lake Michigan, a Lake Michigan much nearer the glacier age, and it was bigger than it would be later on... The lake *did* get smaller as the years went on, didn't it? His mind reeled at the thoughts of receding glaciers and fresh-water lakes and he could see waves moving majestically toward the shore, the gleaming sun reflected from the ever-moving surface and a warm, comfortable feeling came over him as he drifted into sleep.

11

They awakened to a blazing sun and aching bones, the shock of reality staggering their sleepy minds, lying there and looking at each other with wide eyes, daylight filtering through the mound of grass. It wasn't uncomfortable.

Devan was surprised at the deep blue of her eyes because they were so much darker blue than he remembered. Much bluer than Beverly's. And there was always a look of humor about Betty's eyes, as if she were secretly amused at something or might be getting ready to tell you some diverting story. Steady eyes in an oval face, a face he had not seen as close before and he marveled at the smoothness of the skin, the soft appearance of the lips, the little pieces of grass about the face and in the black hair. As he looked at her, she smiled.

"You *are* real, aren't you?" she whispered.

"I hope so. You thought it was a dream, too?"

She nodded, then groaned. "Have you tried to move yet?"

"Afraid to. Think I'll just stay here like this. I can't feel my extremities. I suppose they're still there."

"Maybe we'd be safer if we did stay here. I'd rather, if it's going to be like what was out there last night." She blinked her eyes and they brightened. "I didn't thank you for last night."

She was warm and as she looked at him her eyes widened and then he saw she was looking at his mouth. The grass rustled as she kissed him lightly on the mouth. "Just to let you know I appreciated it," she said. Then she sat up and grass fell in on his face.

His lips burned where she had kissed him. He brought his hand up, brushed the grass to one side and looked up at her.

"Well, what's it like?" The cold of the morning bit his face. He saw her shiver.

"It's no summer day," she said, looking around. "I don't see anybody. Not that I want to see anybody, you understand."

He sat up, could barely see over the top of the dead and bent grass. A few feet behind them the grass ended and the woods began, a thick mass of black bushes and trees. The sky was blue and clean and the sun was warmer than he thought it would be. Before them on the right the grass sloped away to a drop and beyond that they could see the lake. On the left the grass swept upward to the top of the hill.

"Where did they all go?" Devan said.

"You can't see very far."

"I know. What I really meant was that I thought we'd be found. I didn't mean to fall asleep."

"Maybe all the people found their way back through the Needle."

He stood beside her, the ache of suddenly tightened muscles making him grimace and he hid it as best he could because she gave no sign the night on the cold ground had bothered her. Somewhere he had read that women have an extra layer of fat that helps them withstand the cold better than men. He was ready to believe it.

His teeth started to chatter and he mentally upbraided himself for his lack of conditioning. Then he started to shiver and held his breath to stop. He looked at her, saw her breasts rise and fall with regularity. She didn't even have goose pimples. He would have felt better if she had. Suddenly he was aware that his fillings were gone and that his teeth were beginning to ache where the fillings had been.

"Have you figured it out, Dev?" she said, turning to him. "Do you know where we are?"

"Your guess is as good as mine. We came through the Needle with a lot of people. Forward or backward in time or something."

"I'd give everything I own for a good cup of coffee. Maybe it would clear away the cobwebs."

"I'll take ham and eggs and toast—"

"Stop it, Dev! It's hard enough being famished without being reminded of it."

"Sorry. Well, we can't stand here all morning. But I'm not moving without some sort of weapon." He started through the grass to the trees.

"Wait." Betty came toward him. "If we're going to move around we might... well, we might meet someone and..."

He shared her embarrassment momentarily. "All my lounging robes and bathrobes are at the laundry," he said. "But I know what you mean. We'll have to do something."

He moved over the ground littered with old limbs, chose one that felt good to him, returned to where Betty was arranging a skirt of grass — long strands of dry grass over a small branch she had circled her waist with. A few strands were tied about the two ends that met at her side.

"It's not much," she said. "But maybe it will work. At least in case we meet somebody."

"If you can dress for breakfast, so can I." Devan made a skirt of his own.

"Beautiful," she said. "The latest in men's wear. I like the weave."

He picked up his club, balanced it in his hand, made a few practice swings. "If men are going to return to the Stone Age, we'll have to return there, too."

"I think I'd feel better with one of those too," Betty said. "It's not that I don't have confidence in you, Dev, but I just want to make sure. Let's be practical. Two against one is better than ending up with some atavist who doesn't believe in skirts."

When they reached the edge of the slope to the beach and could look down it, they stopped. There were several bodies there, some out of the water, others partway in, moving in rhythm with the waves. The beach was covered with footprints, but no living person was in sight.

They went down to the beach, walked along the shore, making detours around the people lying there. Devan recognized none of the dead people except one.

He pointed to the shriveled body of an old man lying in the shallow water.

"Spencer O'Grady," he said. "A member of the board of directors. Too old to make it, I guess."

"Hideous." Betty turned away.

"I wonder if Dr. Costigan and any of the others made it."

"Where are they? Surely—"

Devan glanced at her quickly, saw her staring at the sky, looked there himself. Smoke from a fire was curling upward at some distance beyond the crest of the distant hill.

"Somebody must be a Boy Scout," Betty said. "Maybe they're cooking breakfast and we'll be just in time. Let's go."

He put a restraining hand on her arm. "Not too fast. If they can turn savage as fast as they did last night, they can turn cannibal just as easy."

When they topped the rise, they found another hill to go over before they could see the fire itself. Still not a sign of anyone. Devan thought it was odd there would be no guard or someone to sound an alarm.

"Dev!" Betty pulled his arm and he whirled, bringing his club up ready for use. She was pointing to the ground and he tried to find the snake she was so upset about. He could see nothing except the grass and a wild flower or two.

"Isn't it strange!" She knelt in the grass, put her face close to a flower growing there.

"What's so amazing about a flower?"

"This is a claytonia virginica-spring beauty to you. Only it isn't, Dev. Instead of having five petals, the flowers are all six-petaled. Don't you see?"

He knelt down and examined the fragile pink blossoms on the eight-inch stem. It didn't seem the slightest bit unusual to him. "Ever hear of a four-leaf clover?"

"Now you're being funny." She looked around the ground. "I know my flowers, Dev, and that's a spring beauty or I'm a dead duck. Only it's different from any I've ever seen before. The soil here is pretty sandy for spring beauties."

"Maybe in prehistoric times spring beauties had six petals."

"Maybe in prehistoric times men had three heads." She got up. "Do you really think we're in prehistoric times?"

"I don't know. All I know is we'd better find out who made that fire. I'm getting hungrier by the minute."

Betty was hesitant to leave her flower. "This makes me feel different. It makes me feel this place is *alien.*"

They started once more toward the top of the hill. Suddenly a loud whooping and hollering arose from beyond it and Devan could hear people running. He put his hand out to stop Betty, then moved in front of her, taking the stance of a man ready to fight for his life and the life of his mate.

Miss Beatrice Treat came running lightly over the hill, saw them and stopped in surprise. She was dressed in a branch and grass that hung like Christmas tree tinsel from it. She finally managed to say, "Mr. Traylor! For Heaven's sake!" Then she rushed down the hill toward them.

"What in the world are you doing with that club?" She looked beyond him to Betty. Devan could tell she was comparing the fashion of the hour, knowing she came off only second best.

"This," Devan said, "is Mrs. Peredge. Beatrice Treat."

The girls exchanged lukewarm greetings.

"Mrs. Peredge is-was Dr. Costigan's secretary," he explained. "Where did you come from?"

She pointed over the hill. "We're all back there-or rather *were* back there. We all just received our work orders. Isn't this fascinating?"

"Work orders?" Betty asked.

"Yes. I've got to hurry."

"Hurry for what?"

"I've got to dig some bulbs, Mr. Traylor. The Indians used to eat them. Didn't you know that?"

"No." He shook his head.

"Really, I've got to move." Miss Treat turned and ran quickly away.

"Things aren't as bad as they were last night, evidently," Betty said. "There's some sort of organization at work, anyway."

They started once more toward the top of the hill, but before they got to the top of it, Devan stopped, turned Betty toward him. "One thing," he said.

"Yes?"

"I don't know what's going to happen when we get over the hill, but I want you to know I want us to be together. I don't know when, how or if we'll ever get back, but until we do get back, I want you with me."

"I was hoping you'd say that."

She didn't object when he took her face in his hands and kissed her.

At the top of the hill they looked down a slope to a natural saucerlike area in the center of which smoldered the remains of a large bonfire. They saw the small group near the fire turn to look at them.

"Devan Traylor!" one of the party yelled, starting toward them. In a moment Devan could see that it was Orcutt, an Orcutt minus his expensive tweeds and smoking pipe, but Orcutt nonetheless in a grass skirt, his body still large and impressive without clothes and held as erect as ever. Others of the group trailed after him.

"Where have you been?" Orcutt said, grabbing his hand, squeezing it hard and pumping it for all it was worth. "We thought you didn't make it." He glanced at Betty. "How are you, Mrs. Peredge? Glad you two came through all right."

"I'll be damned!" It was Sam Otto, his round face illuminated with cheer and sunshine. What Devan first thought was a cigar in his mouth proved to be a stubby branch. "Thought you drowned. Where did you—Oh!" He looked at Betty. "I see. Leave it to you, old Devan boy! We see now what kept him, don't we folks?" He laughed.

Betty blushed all over, blushed even deeper when she realized this. She was about to say something when newcomers — Homer Parrett, Dr. Costigan, James Holcombe, Howard Tooksberry and others — had to shake hands all around.

"Glenn Basher!" Devan caught sight of the man off to one side. "You did come through!"

"Right you are." Basher grinned. "Thought nobody was coming after me for a while. Then all of a sudden I hit the jackpot."

"Detective Griffin...?"

"He's around."

"We're the planning committee, Devan."

"Better not be wasting time," Tooksberry said. "There's lots to do. It may turn cold."

"Who's in charge? You, Orcutt?"

"Well, temporarily, Dev."

After greetings had been extended all around, the group walked back to the clearing.

"As near as we can figure it out," Orcutt told Devan, "about two blocks all the way around the building was affected by the sudden charge of electricity through the Needle. At least that's where the people we've talked to have told us they live. Nobody beyond about a thousand feet or so. Some were riding in cars, others were in bed, in the bathtub, eating, praying, shaving, sleeping — we've had all kinds of activities that were ended by the sudden dropping into the lake."

"Tell him about Eric Sudduth," Basher said. "He'll get a kick out of that."

Orcutt laughed, then sobered. "We shouldn't think it's funny. Those people take it all very seriously."

"It's indecent. That's what it is." Devan looked to see who the voice belonged to and saw Mrs. Charles Petrie attired in a grass skirt and a grass stole that unfortunately only drew attention to what she was trying to conceal. "They'll catch their death of cold, too. How can they live like that?"

"Eric Sudduth and his bunch!" Tooksberry said disgustedly.

"When we all got out of the water last night and shook ourselves off on the beach," Orcutt said, "we saw the glow of this fire. So we all came up here."

"I kept the wood ready," Basher said. "Figured maybe a plane would come by. I practiced making the fire by friction and when we heard the splashes and all the commotion last night, we knew something had happened, so I lighted the fire."

Devan decided it had been started after his tussle with the man on the beach and his escape to the safety of the grass with Betty. Because everybody had gone to the fire, he and Betty had not been discovered.

"It was pretty awful at first," Orcutt said. "Everybody was edging around trying to get close to the fire and some people almost got pushed into it. Lieutenant Johnson and the four policemen got things in hand, though, and restored order. We got people to sit in a large circle, several deep, and we built the fire up so everybody could get warm. We didn't think it would be a good idea if everybody had a fire. It's pretty grassy around here.

"First thing we had to do was stop teeth from aching. We found a retired dentist in the crowd, a Dr. Van

Ness. Lot of people seemed to know him. Anyway, he said to put clay in the holes where the fillings used to be, so you might try that, if you have fillings gone. It stopped my trouble. Dr. Van Ness is out now looking for beeswax. He says that will give us more permanent comfort. So much for teeth. After that we had a council of war—war against whatever we'd find around here, although we haven't found anything yet."

"I found something," Betty said. When they looked at her, she said, "A six-pointed spring beauty." When nobody said anything, she went on, "Maybe you don't know how unusual that is."

"You mean back where we came from they didn't have six petals, is that it?"

Betty nodded. "They had only five. Maybe everything else is like that around here."

"Well, we'll see as time goes on," Orcutt said. "But to get back, we tried to organize everybody into teams. We needed some people to gather wood, others to gather food, others to plan for the next day, and so on."

"It was a matter of 'root hog or die,'" Tooksberry said. "And it's easier if everybody cooperates."

"Everything was coming along good," Orcutt continued, "until Eric Sudduth got up and railed at us for going against what he described as 'God's will.' That was just as we were setting up a committee on clothes."

"Yes," Mrs. Petrie said. "He said if it hadn't been for God's will we wouldn't be here. He said if God intended for us to come here with clothes He'd have provided them. He kept talking about this being

Heaven and about him going away to worship Him. He talked some of the folks into going with him."

"They didn't leave until sunup, though." Dr. Costigan chuckled. "They took advantage of the fire as long as they could."

"But imagine them wanting to run around in nothing but their birthday suits!" Mrs. Petrie said.

Orcutt shrugged. "There are only thirty of them. We have enough to worry about without worrying about them too. We have three hundred and twenty-eight without them, counting you two."

"You think Sudduth will give us any trouble?"

"Not unless he and his acolytes get awfully hungry or cold or something. But look, Dev, we are in the middle of planning things and we can use you. Know anything about hunting or fishing or trapping? That's what we need right now."

"I didn't see any animals," Devan said. "Are you sure there are some around?"

"They've been scared away again," Basher said. "They were frightened when I first showed up and didn't come back for several hours. You want to be prepared, though."

"Why?"

"The rabbits aren't exactly rabbits. Their ears aren't so long and their tails aren't powder puffs. More like cat tails."

"Can they be trapped?"

"I don't know. We'll have to find out."

"Basher's been living on reindeer moss and lichens," Orcutt said. "Tried to catch fish but couldn't.

Now we have things more or less organized. We'll have fish before you know it."

"We saw Miss Treat running to do her job," Betty said. "She's got to dig up bulbs, she said. She told us Indians used to eat them."

"I'm no authority," Orcutt said. "A couple Boy Scouts came through the Needle and they're up on their Indian lore. A couple other people who've been helpful are the Navy and Army men who took survival courses. It's all organized. We've got one group burying the dead, another fishing in the lake, trying to catch fish with their hands, another group making fish nets out of some of the saplings—that will be only temporary, though.

"The people here early this morning joined whatever group they felt best fitted for. An ex-undertaker is heading up the burial detail, for example. Miss Treat is with the group looking for edible roots, bulbs and grubs. Another is looking for watercress and skunk cabbage and squirrel caches of walnuts, butternuts and hickory nuts. Basher says he thinks he saw a squirrel or two before we all dropped in on him, didn't you?"

"Yes, I did," Basher said. He hesitated, then added, "They were white, the three I saw, in case you want to know."

"There's another group out looking for stones we can use for hammers and axes and for flint. We've got to make a tinderbox. Still another party's out getting fallen logs together for lean-tos and another group is sharpening fallen branches as best they can in the hopes they can bag something with spears. We won't starve."

Devan grunted. "Sounds to me as if everything is under control."

"Right now it is, Dev. Food is our most vital need now and always. As soon as that's taken care of, then we can start thinking about such things as how to prepare it, how to build real shelters, how to care for the people medically and dentally. It's going to be some job. Where do you want to fit in? I'd like to have you with me, if you don't mind. I've always admired you and I think a few of us could run this show. Besides, I've got your job already picked out. The most important one of all."

"The most important? What's that?"

Orcutt grinned at him. "You're the engineer, aren't you?"

"One of them. But there's no need for much engineering right now that I can see."

"Maybe not right now, but there will be later."

"Still don't understand. Housing won't take much engineering, especially electronics engineering."

"You want to get back, don't you?"

"Sure, but what's that got to do with it?"

"We can't get back through the Needle that got us here."

"That's right," Dr. Costigan said. "The pipe Blaine tossed wrecked all the circuits. I imagine some of the coils just melted together."

"So?"

"So we build another Needle, Devan," Orcutt said.

12

Devan laughed at the thought of building a Needle in the wilderness in which they found themselves. It would be impossible. To build a Needle takes electricity, lathes, forgings, wire, radio tubes, a million and one things. Orcutt should have known that.

"Where would you get the iron, Ed? Just answer me that."

"I don't know the answer any more than you do, Dev. All I know is I want to go home and so does everybody else and another Needle's the only way I can think of doing it."

"But iron!"

"Hell, we're not savages, Devan, are we? When we came to this place we didn't revert back. We still have our minds. All we need is a blast furnace, some iron ore and a fire, isn't it?"

Devan laughed again. A blast furnace, indeed! Then the thought of it sobered him and brought him face to face with the fact that home and Beverly and the children were far, far away. Years away. He shuddered and the remembrance filled him with a loneliness he hadn't known for years. It was while he was thinking nostalgically of familiar faces and rooms and chairs and streets, and realizing that they would have aged by many months before he would ever see them again, that he saw Betty looking at him with the same expression he must have had. To see her made him feel less lonely and he felt a kinship with her because she, too, realized they would be here a long time. He was glad they had agreed to be together.

"Orcutt's right about iron," he told Betty when they went on a trip to the beach to pick up shells that might be sharpened into usefulness. "Not just for the Needle. We'll need it for everything else."

He told her that iron was more valuable than gold. But then, it was at home, too, wasn't it? You could take all the gold and throw it away and who would miss it? The men guarding the vaults at Fort Knox, the dentists, metallurgists, manufacturers and jewelers. But if you took iron away, it would be the end of civilization. No more stainless steel, scissors, cars, motors, airplanes, knives, guns, skyscrapers. The list was endless. He knew the metal was versatile. It could be one of the toughest or one of the most brittle, strong or weak, magnetic or not, soft or hard—it all depended on what you mixed it with and how you stirred the pot.

"I see why you're an engineer," Betty said. "You talk about things like that as if there wasn't anything else in the world. You love your work, don't you?"

"Of course. Just as you do your flowers."

"You'll build another Needle."

He stood for a moment looking out over the lake, at the choppy waves, the horizon. "Yes," he said. "I think I will."

"It will take years, though." Suddenly she stooped down, picked up the bones of a fish. She laughed. "Look. Does your engineering mind tell you what this is? I'll bet not. It would take a woman to figure this out. See my pins? I've got thorns and here are fishbones. I'm going to do a consumer report on which makes the better pin."

"We don't need anyone to invent the safety pin," he said. "Had you thought of that?"

"We could use a chemist, though."

"That's not all. How about a doctor?"

"I noticed the women. They came through, unborn babies and all. Didn't you see them?"

"Yes," he said. "I noticed the women. One in particular." He grinned at her. She was pretty, standing there, her toes in the sand, the wind blowing her black hair about her bare shoulders; she was lovely, a vision, smaller than he but not fragile. There was something appealing about her posture, in the round line of her breast, the gentle curve of her hips, something challenging about her glance. He met the challenge and she was warm and soft and pliable in his arms.

Later, they sat on rocks and looked out over the water.

"It's beyond imagination what needs to be done, isn't it? We haven't even a penknife to start with."

"You mentioned a doctor awhile ago. What good would he be without chemicals? Nothing for his hypodermic. In fact, no hypodermic."

"He'll get his hypodermic when you make iron and glass."

"And the chemicals?"

The stones were cold and, when they were inactive, so was the air. "Let's not worry about it," she said. "At least the doctor can tell you what kind of a disease you have. As far as the prescription goes, this will undoubtedly go down in history as the era of the placebo."

When everyone gathered about the new fire in the clearing shortly before what appeared to be noon, Devan saw that the women had followed Mrs. Petrie's example and were wearing stoles and new grass skirts. Both were much more functional than those worn earlier in the day, which had been made before daylight.

There was a spread of fish on the grass and the men explained that some had been caught by hand and others by several small nets made of young saplings. Miss Treat displayed a row of bulbs and grubs and was highly pleased when Howard Tooksberry complimented her on her morning's work. Lieutenant Johnson and several of his men had brought down about twenty rabbits, which were being prepared for the spits with sharpened shells and rocks. There were mounds of nuts here and there, some collected by eager youngsters who now danced around them, hardly able to wait for the eating.

The scene gave Devan a start. It reminded him of the primitive tableaux in the Field Museum in Chicago.

He was surprised to find how satisfied his appetite was after the meal. There was no salt or pepper, no bread, nothing except a piece of rabbit, a small fish, some nuts and watercress. Yet, when it all was washed down with water picked up by cupped hands from a nearby spring that fed the lake, he felt whole again.

Later Orcutt mounted a pile of logs that had been dragged to the site from the forest, held his hands in the air for silence and then Devan knew how the organization in the middle of the night had been formed. Despite the white stubble of a beginning beard and the white hair, Orcutt's black brows and flashing eyes demanded attention; he was still a commanding figure.

Orcutt explained that, because some food was left, fewer people were needed on the food-gathering units. He asked for volunteers for a canoe-making detail, a group to look for sugar maple trees, some women to experiment with clay for pottery and others to try their hands at weaving. He directed the men working with the logs to erect lean-tos in a circle around the clearing, some small and some large, depending on the size of families.

It was satisfying, having a man of Orcutt's caliber directing the labors, Devan thought. He looked around at the many faces, did not see the men he had encountered the previous night on the beach; they must have belonged to the group that went with Eric Sudduth, he decided.

When night came and they built up the fire, the group from the Needle experiment sat together, first warming one side of their bodies, then the other. Some of the others sat near by, though most family groups had carried burning twigs to start fires in front of their lean-tos.

"Sure it's the same sky," Orcutt was saying. "There's the Dipper and the Milky Way and—well, you can *tell* it is."

"Yes, but what year is it?" Basher asked.

"It must be thousands of years ago." Sam Otto turned his body around. "Otherwise there'd be Indians around."

"Anybody know anything about stars?" Orcutt asked the question of everyone within hearing distance.

A man twenty feet away heard him, came over. "I know a little bit about 'em," he said. He was a tall man with stooped shoulders and no teeth, a mere shadow of a man, considering his weight. Devan wondered how he ever survived the transition.

"My name's Elmo Hodge. I used to manage that grocery store right down the street from your place. Astronomy's my hobby." He sat down. "You'll have to bear with me a little. My teeth didn't come with me. What do you want to know about the stars?"

"The stars move, don't they?" Orcutt asked.

The man nodded. "Ever so little."

"Enough to tell us how far back into time we went when we went through the Needle?"

Mr. Hodge looked at Orcutt for a long time, then he looked at the others in growing amazement.

"You mean you don't know?"

"Know what?" Betty's hand tightened around Devan's.

"Only a day has gone by since we came through the Needle."

Devan's hopes for information sank. The man didn't know what he was talking about. Nobody wanted to start an argument. Nobody wanted the old man to feel bad, so they didn't tell him how wrong he was.

"I know what you're all thinkin'," he said. "But it just isn't so." He pointed to the north. "See the Big Dipper? Now. Starting with the stars in the handle, the first one is moving down, the second is moving to the left as are all of them except the one on the lip of the Dipper. It's moving down just like the first one. If this were any other time, the Dipper'd be all out of shape. It looks pretty much as it always has, doesn't it?"

"A thousand years." The gravel voice of Clarence Gleckman boomed from the edge of the circle of faces. "A thousand years wouldn't make much difference."

Hodge frowned a little, nodded his head again. "You're right, there. A thousand years wouldn't do much. It would take a hundred thousand years to make a big difference."

"Then how do you know you're right?" Orcutt said.

"All right," Hodge said. "Look at Saturn. Right at the edge of Virgo and near to Libra. Just as it was early last night, if my eyes serve me right, right there on the horizon." He studied the stars for a few minutes, scowling. Then he said, "I'll wager you'll find the North Star still the North Star. A few thousand years ago Alpha Draconis was the Pole Star, just as Vega will be the North Star in twelve thousand years."

"Well, there's no doubt about one thing," Devan said. "You know your stars."

"Seems to me I've heard about that somewhere," Holcombe said. "It sounds right."

"I think so, too," Tooksberry added.

"I don't care about the stars," Mrs. Petrie said. "I looked at them often enough when I was a girl. What I want right now is some yarn. My fingers are itching for some knitting to do."

"We'll put you on weaving as soon as somebody builds a loom," Orcutt said.

Hodge cleared his throat. "Another thing. If we get any glass made, I'll grind lenses for telescopes. I've made hundreds of them. With the first one I'll take a look at Castor. It's a double star and they're getting about as close as they'll ever be, if time hasn't changed. And I don't think it has. Oh, there's plenty of proof up there," he said, pointing to the sky, "if you care to look for it."

"So no time has gone by." Dr. Costigan was staring into the fire. He sighed. "Imagine that."

"Well," Miss Treat said by way of getting attention. Devan was pleased to see she was with Tooksberry. "If this isn't some *other* time... Am I being silly?"

"Not at all, my dear." Tooksberry patted her hand and smiled up at her and she beamed at him in return. "It's a perfectly good question. If this isn't *then*, how can it be *now* and not Chicago?"

"That is a good question," Orcutt said.

"I once read a story about identical worlds that existed both at the same time, both occupying the same space," Basher said. "It was some years ago. The idea was that there were supposed to be an infinite number of possible worlds and if you knew how you could jump from one to the other and find yourself in the same place but in a different possibility."

"Fantastic," Tooksberry said.

"Instead of trying to figure out where we are," Mrs. Petrie said, "let's begin by admitting we're here and then figure out how we can get back to where we were."

"We're going to make another Needle," Devan said. "But it's going to take a long time. We've got to mine iron ore and make a blast furnace and set up all the processes for everything we're going to need."

"It will be a tremendous job," Dr. Costigan said.

"That's not all that's going to be laborious," Orcutt said, winding a tough length of grass around a branch. "What if we can't make a Needle?" He looked up at the faces. "We might as well face it. Suppose we've forgotten some industrial process? We know it exists, but we don't know how to go about solving it because we haven't anyone in our group who has had any experience or training in that line. What then?"

"We'll work around it," Basher said. "Just as during the war you couldn't get certain kinds of radio tubes so you revised the circuit to accommodate what tubes were available."

"Maybe. All right. Suppose we have a Needle built. Where do we know it's going to take us when we walk into it? Just as you say, Basher, maybe it will take us into another possible world, one different from our own and different from this one. Maybe one inhabited by beings different from us."

"I've thought of that," Dr. Costigan said. "And I think I've got the answer. If we make another Needle, it's going to be just like the one we made. I can tell you that the part that energized the units that created the force field that brought us here was powered by direct current. So I think if we reversed polarity—just reversed the wires on the input side—we'd create a field that would take us back."

"I don't know about you people," Mrs. Petrie said, "but I'm going to get some sleep. I'm not accustomed to moving around so much as I have today. Good night."

"One cigarette," said Lieutenant Johnson after Mrs. Petrie had gone. He had been sitting near by all the while. "Just one cigarette. That's all. That's the thing I miss most. You wouldn't think a little thing like that would ever get such a hold on you, would you?"

"It's a filthy habit," Devan said, "and I love it."

Betty punched him in the ribs. "Me, too."

"We might be able to find the tobacco leaf around here somewhere," Dr. Costigan said.

"Personally, I'll take a pipe," Orcutt said. "You can have your cigarettes."

"You fellows don't know what you're talking about," Sam Otto said. "Cigarettes are a sissy smoke. Cigars are the only smokes."

"You'd get about the same pleasure out of an old twig," Devan said. "You never light one anyway."

Dr. Costigan put his hands up for silence. "Gentlemen," he said gravely. "There is something even more important than tobacco. It is the grape. And I plan to find a wild grapevine somewhere. What would life be without the wassail bowl?"

It was only a small shelter, grass-covered logs and limbs set at an angle on a crossbeam which rested on large branches that had been forced into the moist earth. They had gathered considerable grass for the floor and more for a covering.

That and the fire in front of the lean-to gave them a fair degree of comfort.

"Will we ever get back, Devan?"

Betty was lying on her stomach, looking into the fire, her hair blowing a little in the breeze as it swept by, her chin on her folded arms. There was something moist about the spring-night breeze, something that gave promise of blooms to come. There was, too, the odor of many fires which flickered and lighted the area, the air sounding with the cracking and popping of burning firewood. Devan was tired and sleepy.

"I don't know, Betty. We haven't even started yet. We've got to start from scratch and even surviving against such odds would be problematical for city folks like us, much less working out a highly intricate problem like Costigan's Needle. There are other things, too."

"Such as?" She turned on her side to look at him.

"We'll need paper to write the problems down on, for Dr. Costigan to record his diagrams. Have you thought of what would happen if he died? We'd never get back then."

"I hadn't thought of it."

"And the electricity. How are we going to get that?"

"You'll do it."

"And then the final thing."

"The final thing?"

"It's all right for Dr. Costigan to say he'll reverse the polarity and we'll get back, but supposing we reverse the polarity and go somewhere else? What then?"

Betty sighed. "Maybe Mr. Sudduth is right after all. Maybe we should just relax and say God put us here and it's up to Him to take care of us. Maybe we're just creating trouble and worry."

Devan shook his head. "I don't think Sudduth is right. There is the admonishment that God helps those who help themselves. If we don't help ourselves, if we don't have a goal, if we aren't busy—then we're in trouble. What would have happened if Orcutt hadn't taken over and organized things and given us a goal?"

"It would have been ghastly."

13

A bright June sun made rocks hot and a warm breeze whispered among new leaves and spring flowers nodded their heads pleasantly. Everywhere in the long expanse of sometimes sand, sometimes woods and everywhere grass, except within a few hundred feet of the lake's edge, there was activity. There was much to be done in the spring and summer.

Birds up from the deep south were busy in the trees and their distant relatives, the prairie chickens and grouse, were just as busy in the fields. Beaver came out of lodges and looked over the situation around the rivers, their eyes on water levels—and other beaver. Turkeys strutted around, and for foxes and wolves the long winter and hunger was at an end.

At one spot, almost insignificant in the area at the lake, there was much activity, too. It was marked by rising columns of smoke from several of the many log and brick buildings in a large settlement. These long plumes of smoke came, for the most part, from chimneys over fireplaces where, a short time before, dinner had been cooked. Now the men had gone back to their work in the fields, in the woods, in the building in the stockade, and the women, their noontime labors soon over, would go back to their special occupations at spinning wheels, looms, or in kindergarten and school-rooms.

There was one large cloud of smoke that rose lazily that came from no fireplace. It lifted from a particular spot inside the settlement on the north side where Devan Traylor, sweat trickling down his dusty, dirt-streaked face into his leather jacket, worked bellows with a frantic urgency.

"We don't have to kill ourselves," a large, blond man at a nearby bellows said, his bulging muscles working it without seeming effort. "We'll get enough air there. Those clay passages are just right. They'll by-pass the stuff that falls down."

"All right, Gus," Devan said, between gulps of air. "We don't want to get the iron so hot it'll go down it-self. You ought to know what you're doing."

Gus Nelson grinned good-naturedly. "I didn't get too close to the furnaces at Gary," he said, "but I knew more than they thought I did. As long as we don't get it too hot, we're all right. Here, let me handle both bel-lows. We don't need so much air, now that we got it started good."

Devan stepped back thankfully, eyed the furnace speculatively. "Need any more charcoal, Gus, do you think?"

The big man spat on the ground. "Naw. Oh, I don't know. You might put on a little of everything. Not more than one load, though."

Devan scooped up a shovelful of charcoal, threw it on the pile of incandescence, did the same with the red ore and limestone. When he offered to have a go at the bellows, the massive man shook his head and smiled.

This would be the best iron that Devan and Gus had so far made. At first Devan had appealed for volunteers to find a source of ore and many men stopped what they were doing to join the group which scattered south, east and west, scouring the area for the ore. The first reports only told of the animals they had seen, a few bears which raced into the underbrush at their approach, a few wolves and foxes (one man said he thought he saw a buffalo) and deer.

One man found the Sudduth settlement about twenty miles south of the lake, the inhabitants living in limestone caves. The reporter, who said he didn't get too close, said the Sudduthites were still taking seriously their rule of nudism. He was kidded by friends who asked, since he didn't get too close, just how he knew. Others jokingly said they could understand why he hadn't found any ore.

"There ain't a good-looking one in the bunch," he said.

"He must have looked 'em all over, then," someone else said. Then there was a fight and everybody got in it.

In the end the men found the soft, red ore where they least expected to find it: within a mile of the camp near the surface of the earth. They started to work it opencut fashion, loading it first on wooden sleds they dragged over ground until a cart with wheels could be built.

Devan's first attempt at making iron was made alone in an open pit with ore and charcoal and a brisk north wind to help and Betty to offer encouragement. After several days the fire was allowed to go out and the mass of iron extracted. It was soft and malleable and hardly worth the effort, Devan decided, but it was a start.

Then Gus Nelson, who had been on fishing and hunting trips, stopped one morning to take a look at the ironworks. Gus had been put on the log contingent, but he pleaded for the other work because he had always wanted to hunt and fish and had never done so.

"Why don't you try a blast furnace?" he suggested.

"I'm going to," Devan said. "I only wanted to see what would happen with the simplest outfit. Now I know. It's not good enough."

Devan saw the rippling muscles, the honest blue of his eyes and the strong back. "Why don't you give a guy a hand instead of just standing there full of advice?"

"I think I'd rather fish." His smile was bright.

"So would I. But we need iron. How's fishing?"

"Pretty good."

"It could be better."

"How?"

"Fishhooks. Iron fishhooks." Devan saw the man was interested, followed it up. "We need spears, steel points for arrows. Knives for skinning. Why don't you join up? Traylor and Nelson, the nearest you can get to U. S. Steel this side of the Needle."

The idea appealed to the big man and he went to work. They made bellows out of skins of animals, directed the air into the clay channels beneath the place where they would deposit the charcoal and ore, then went after several loads of ore. Limestone was Gus Nelson's suggestion and Devan remembered it was used to reduce the ore quickly, was glad the man had come around. After the ironworks got started, Devan would give it to him entirely. There were other things needed, too, like glass, wire, electricity. But iron was basic.

Basic. Devan was amused to find how basic women considered cosmetics, which he thought would be one of the last things they would worry about in the wilderness. But rouge and lipstick were important. The women had found certain red-powder deposits just beneath the surface of the ground. It made good rouge. It was some time before the men discovered the women had been getting the powder from the iron ore deposits and that it was, in fact, the same thing and that the women had discovered it first. Cornmeal, chalk, flour, though nothing like the face powder women had been used to, doubled for it. Some of the darker ore, mixed with animal fats, served as a reddish-brown lipstick, though some women objected to the taste. Still, the recollection of what real lipstick looked like fading into dim memory, it looked good. It was good enough for many a maiden to snare a man with.

Basic. The men devoted much of their time to searching for the tobacco plant. When they finally found a patch of it, there were plenty of clay pipes already made and waiting to be filled.

Life on the other side of the Needle, Devan decided, wasn't going to be so different after all.

Devan and Gus watched the rising cloud of smoke emanating from inside the circular wall of clay.

"I remember one time in the plant when there was a leak in one of the furnaces," Gus said, idly eying the mass of dull red inside the shaft. "It wasn't open like this. The gas coming out was carbon monoxide, they said. Anyway, they got everybody away from the furnace until they repaired it."

"There could be carbon monoxide coming out of this thing right now," Devan said. "But I don't think it would hurt anybody. It's too open around here."

"How are the steelmakers?" Betty had walked over to the two men standing by the furnace. "I don't see how you stand it, being so near that heat."

"Used to it," Devan said. "What brings you around?"

"Want to know how big you want those clay boxes."

"You'd better wait until we get the iron out and hammer it into shape."

She put her arm in his. "Is this going to be better than the last?"

"This is going to be tops, Mrs. Traylor," Gus said. "We're going to make carbon steel this time."

"I've heard of that. Stronger than regular, isn't it?"

"There's lots to be done before that, though," Devan said. "As soon as the furnace gets cool enough, we're going to take the iron out—it's going to still be hot. Then"—and he motioned to another bellows-and-fire outfit with a large flat rock and hammer near by— "we're going to hammer it to get out as much slag as possible."

"We ain't got a cinder notch," Gus said. "No iron notch either. Getting it out would be easy that way."

"Then we're going to hammer it into the shape we want. That's where your box comes in. We'll put the items in there, heat them for several days and let them absorb carbon and turn into carbon steel. Simple, isn't it?"

"Sounds simple," she said. "Is that really the way it's supposed to work?"

"That's what Gus says." Devan saw a man come round a corner of a log building and head for them. He recognized the man as Dr. Van Ness. The dentist nodded to them.

"No patients today, Doctor?" Betty asked.

"Know something?" He examined his fingernails, raised his eyebrows. "I don't want to accuse anybody, but since we started administering wine for extractions we have more business than we can take care of."

"We've got troubles of our own," Gus grumbled.

"It's a poor substitute for Novocain, but since Dr. Costigan rations it for extractions, people would rather have their teeth pulled than filled. Making winos out of everybody."

"I need some more fillings, Doctor," Devan said. "When can I come over?"

The dentist sat on a log. "You'll have to see Miss Anderson. She'll tell you when there's free time. But I didn't come over to solicit business. I came over to gripe."

"Gripe? What about?"

"I'm going to have to quit the fillings until I get better equipment."

"What's the trouble with the stuff I made for you?"

"Rather embarrassing." The little man chuckled. "Don't think the patients liked it either. Like a comedy movie. You work around cleaning out a cavity with a spoon extractor, see? Then you are just about through when *bing,* the thing crumbles or bends. The metal's not right. It's happened to every one you made."

"That's why we made so many," Gus said darkly. "We knew they wouldn't last. I thought we told you."

Devan gestured toward the little furnace. "We've got some new stuff in there," he said. "When we get it out, it's going to be different. We're going to work it into the right shape, then impregnate it with carbon. You'll see the difference."

"That's more like it." The dentist brightened.

"You working by yourself, Doctor?"

"Got a couple kids learning the business. I won't last forever, you know. I teach them mostly at night, though." He reached into the pocket of his leather jacket, drew out a piece of parchment. "I've drawn some new instruments here." He pointed to them. "A lancet, if you can do it, scalers, more forceps, elevators, excavators, hand chisels. I need more sizes and shapes, lacking a drill."

"I hope I never have to go to a dentist," Gus said, viewing the illustrations with wide eyes. "I went to one once. That was enough."

"You're just a baby," Dr. Van Ness said. "Lucky your teeth are good. You may be a big man, but you're a baby." When Gus Nelson's face went red, the dentist laughed. "Struck oil, didn't I? I used to never be able to say such things. Now I can. Now I can tell my patients what I think of them."

"You'd better shut up," Gus said.

"What are you going to do when you get all the fillings done?" Devan asked. "Can you make false teeth? A whole set?"

"There'll be enough work for two or three dentists here," the dentist said. "I've got to get more gold, though. Lots of it."

"Why don't you just fill the teeth with some other temporary substance?"

"Some *other* temporary substance?" The dentist was surprised.

"That just goes to show how little people know about dentistry. Gold is the best stuff there is. Damn permanent, too. Dentists would have always used it in preference to anything else but it takes about an hour to fill a cavity with it. They'd have to charge too much. Gold doesn't tarnish or corrode. You roll the gold out and make foil and rope. Nothing can beat it.

"When I fill a tooth, I clean out the hole, let it dry and assist a little with a small bellows. Then I put in a little gold rope, take the six-inch condenser and mallet and I'm on my way."

"It's very interesting, Doctor," Betty said. "I—"

"Do you realize I've got to make sure I don't have less than fifteen pounds of static force on the circular gold condenser point—you know the one you made for me—otherwise the gold won't condense properly?"

"What are you blabbering about, anyway?" Gus asked.

Devan grinned. "He's telling me the magnitude of the impact force, which is proportional to the product of the force exerted and the square of the velocity with which it is applied, should not be less than fifteen pounds."

Gus's mouth dropped open.

"Don't feel bad about it, Gus," Betty said. "I don't understand it either. I'm not so sure Devan did in the first place."

"Ah, you haven't heard anything yet," Dr. Van Ness said, moving back and forth in front of them. "Wait until I start on the dentures. Always wanted to make gold ones. They're the best. Nobody has enough money to buy any back where we come from, except a few. But now I'll be able to do it."

"That's fine, Doctor," Devan said.

"We'll find some gypsum," the doctor went on. "We'll make plaster of Paris, then cast a gold denture with pegs where the teeth ought to be—I'm going to need a set of impression trays, Mr. Traylor. I'll use them with the plaster for the impression of the alveolar arch..." His face beamed. "I can see them now. Gold dentures."

"But what about the teeth?"

The dentist shrugged. "The teeth? I'll carve them. Carve them from animal tusks-there are goats around, aren't there? I don't see any acrylic lying around waiting to be picked up, do you?" He laughed. "God knows it wouldn't make dentures as good anyway. I'll take gold every time. Do you realize a gold denture would cost more than five hundred dollars ordinarily?" He rubbed his hands gleefully. "This will be quite an experiment. Quite an experiment. I only hope the gold holds out."

Orcutt looks good, Devan thought. Better than I've ever seen him. He's got a healthy tan and he's lost that paunch he had. He'd be a magnificent figure of a man if it weren't for that beard of his. It makes him look like a prophet.

"Fine dinner," Orcutt said, tilting his chair back against the front log wall. The leather thongs that held the chair together creaked a little as he did so. He sucked smoke through his clay pipe, exhaled it as if he enjoyed it.

"Sure was," Renthaler said. Renthaler was Walter Renthaler, a sandy-haired, pudgy, cheerful and quick-eyed young man Devan guessed couldn't have been more than twenty-five at the most. Orcutt had brought him to dinner. Said he had something to talk over with Devan.

It would have to be something about chemistry, Devan figured. Renthaler had solved the soap problem for them and endeared himself to the hearts of all the women as a result. It was he who told how water could be run through wood ashes and then through a layer of slaked lime to produce the lye used to make soap. He was an industrial chemist, had been visiting a friend in the neighborhood when displacement occurred for him.

They were sitting just outside in chairs, the flicker of candlelight from inside making a widening swath on the ground. There was a smell of blossoms in the air. Betty could tell what they were, Devan thought, knowing she would be enjoying the fragrance even though she was washing earthenware dishes behind the log house.

"Lucky for us Walter came through," Orcutt said. "He's going to show us the way."

"Don't put it that way, Mr. Orcutt," Renthaler said. "I happened to specialize in the candy field. But I do know a little general chemistry that might come in handy."

"You know more than a little the way you were talking to me about it," Orcutt said. He turned to Devan. "I want you to hear what Walter's got to say. The point of it all you might not get at first, so I'll tell you. We've considered glass, haven't we?"

"Yes. That and batteries, radios, refrigerators, gasoline motors, electric devices—"

"Okay." Orcutt tapped his clay pipe lightly on his leather sandal. "Why go back to the old ways? Sure, we'll make glass, but we won't specialize in it. No use going through the Bronze Age if we have something better than bronze."

"We've got to think of the Needle," Devan reminded him.

"Of course. I realize the Needle comes first. But it's going to take years."

"We may never get back if Dr. Costigan doesn't leave the grapes alone and start drawing some diagrams."

"He's waiting on you," Orcutt said. "Now Walter here is going to make everything out of plastics. Just think of that! Here we are pioneers, but we're going to get plastics. You tell him, Walter. Devan will provide whatever you need in the way of steel."

"Gus Nelson will," Devan said. "I'm turning over the steel mill to him as soon as it gets rolling. But what do you want to say, Walter?"

"Well, you're probably familiar with the fact that lots of stuff men threw away for years is useful."

"You mean like coal-tar products, corn products."

"That's right. We can make plates, cups, saucers, glasses, tubes—the list is endless, Mr. Traylor." Renthaler was a little shy. His voice was soft, his manner courteous.

"Just how would you go about making plastics out here in the woods?" Devan asked with what he thought was just the right provocative tone, filling his own clay pipe while Renthaler gave him a sharp look.

"I'll get a light," Orcutt said, disappearing inside.

"Casein," Renthaler said, "can be made from sour milk and formaldehyde. Cellulose acetate from cotton linters with acetic acid used in the presence of a catalyst—sulphuric acid. Maybe the best bet would be phenol-formaldehyde resin. It might be the easiest."

Devan grinned. "Where would we get the phenol?"

"Fractional distillation of coal."

"You need glass for that."

"It isn't the best method. There are many."

"How about formaldehyde?"

"It can be made by oxidizing methyl alcohol."

"Oh, fine. Where do we get the methyl alcohol?"

"It's wood alcohol. Just heat wood—we've got beech and birch, they're the best—in the absence of air."

"Distillation again, eh?"

Renthaler shrugged. "Oh, it won't be easy, but it makes more sense to work in that direction than it does in others. The advantages of plastic containers over glass ones ought to be obvious."

"I'm sure they are."

"Your wife ought to be out back with plastic dishes."

Devan laughed. "It doesn't make sense, does it? Pioneering the way we are and getting plastics. It's an anachronism!"

"If we can get soy beans, corn and cotton, we'll really be set, Mr. Traylor."

"In more ways than one, I'd say, Walter."

"I'm visualizing polystyrene, vinyl resinoids, nylon, rayon, synthetic rubber. It will be wonderful working it all out."

In Renthaler's eyes Devan saw the same look he had seen in Dr. Van Ness's eyes. The eagerness, the curiosity, the interest and the patience. Yes, as long as there were men like that around there would eventually be a Needle. Devan felt sure of that.

Orcutt came out with a lighted stick and both men lit their pipes.

"I'll help you all I can," Devan said. "You let me know what you need. I'm going to work on glass with Glenn Basher next. Maybe you'd like to help me with that. If you would, it would hurry up your project all the more."

"We're making a lot of progress, gentlemen," Orcutt said, putting his hands behind his head. "Paper mill's coming along."

"I wondered how that was doing," Renthaler said. "Are you still going to ask everybody to write down all the poems he knows?"

Orcutt nodded absently, looking up into the night sky. "Yes, everything anybody has memorized. Plots, too. The great stories. We want them written down somewhere. Just in case we never get back. We will have something to preserve."

"You're joking," Renthaler said. "We'll get back. We have the man who invented the Needle, haven't we? He ought to get us back."

"We'll see," Orcutt said. "Let's hope he can do it."

14

Though Eric Sudduth and his followers kept pretty much to themselves in their caves a good twenty miles south of New Chicago, they were often the subject of conjecture and conversation. After all, the area served as a source of limestone for the smelting works and other processes and as the home of the only neighbors the New Chicagoans were apparently ever to have.

When parties from New Chicago went out to hunt deer, they invariably skirted the Sudduthite area, but always made certain they got close enough to see if any changes had been made. Their reports were relayed to Orcutt; they usually consisted of assurances that the Sudduthites had not changed their minds about clothes, that they had fires, that they had made weapons to kill wild animals and protect themselves from an occasional wolf.

The reports brought back by the hunters were neither as clear nor as complete as the ones delivered in person by the couples who returned from the outlander camp requesting sanctuary (Sudduth had ordered death for deserters) and permanent residence in New Chicago—or residence until the new Needle was

developed and they could return home. All were surprised that another Needle was in prospect.

By mid-June, three couples had come back and the
reason was quite simple: the women had become
pregnant, did not like the idea of parturition in such
primeval surroundings. At least that was the obvious
reason; it may be that they had some idea of what a
winter could be like without clothes in a drafty cave, or
they may have heard that two young men, both of
whom had been interns at the time of the displacement, were doing a good job taking care of the medical
and surgical needs of New Chicago. The latter was
doubtful, however, because Sudduth professed no interest in what went on up north and his cohorts, with
discretion, followed his example.

The six were quickly and effortlessly absorbed into
New Chicago and were given jobs in line with their
past experience, ability and desires. In return, three
small brick cottages were built for them inside the big
enclosure and their previous identity with the other
group was quickly forgotten.

From what they told of Sudduth and his assistant
director, Orvid Blaine, the New Chicagoans began to
get a picture of what was going on in the south. As was
believed, Sudduth and Blaine were the leaders of the
group, directed all the activities and established all the
policies. Devan was sorry to hear that the men held the
people in virtual enslavement, demanding the best of
the food and not lifting a finger to do anything themselves.

They said that Sudduth had issued an order which stated that, since he was the spiritual head of the group, he could have any woman in the clan he wanted. He was so convincing in his arguments with those who opposed the directive, the story went on, that he almost swayed the husbands and wives to his desires. But the first woman he wanted was Blaine's and, in the ensuing struggle which ended with Sudduth giving in to Blaine, the plan fell through and the man knew better than to try to make stick for someone else what he couldn't make stick for his assistant.

Devan had heard Orcutt voice concern over the fact that the emigrants meant Sudduth's numbers were down to twenty-four, beside himself and Blaine, and that Sudduth might try to take back those who had decided to move to New Chicago.

"He's sure to try something," Orcutt said. "He won't just sit by and let his people drift up here."

It followed, then, that when Eric Sudduth and his assistant presented themselves at the New Chicago gate in mid-summer, it did not come too much as a surprise.

"Anybody home?" They could hear Sudduth's thunderous roar and Blaine in the background throughout the whole camp. There was no denying it, Eric Sudduth was an impressive man, the kind of man with whom there could be no middle ground. Either you liked him and did whatever he said and believed his every word and considered him a great man, or you hated him right from the start because you could see how he could use you and your friends for himself.

Devan disliked him, was certain Orcutt and others felt the same way.

When several persons had run and told Orcutt that Sudduth was at the gate, though he didn't need to be told because there was nothing wrong with his ears, Orcutt sighed and went there, taking Devan and Sam Otto with him, mostly because he met them on the way. He stopped for a moment to see Tooksberry en route.

When the big gate swung open, the trio was surprised to find Sudduth and Blaine standing there naked, for they had momentarily forgotten the precept embraced by the Sudduthites. Their bodies were remarkably white and pasty in contrast to the bronzed skin of the New Chicagoans. The reason for this, Devan decided, was that these two had done no work, had been waited on hand and foot, had lived too much in caves. He wondered what their constituents looked like and guessed they were worked pretty hard satisfying their leaders, judging by the pot belly Sudduth had. Devan hadn't remembered that it was that big. Blaine either had not eaten so much or had not advanced to the age where, if he did, it would show after a while.

Seeing the three New Chicagoans in leather jackets and knee-length trousers and freshly shaved, the two naked men, who had chest-length white beards, seemed ill at ease and much less sure of themselves than they had sounded before the gate was opened. They stood now, looking a little ridiculous, Devan thought, twenty feet from the gate where the brush and trees began.

Eric Sudduth drew his shoulders back and achieved something of a look of dignity. He cleared his throat. "You have six of my people here," he said. "Mr. Blaine and I have come to take them back with us."

Orcutt smiled and when he did Devan was filled with a confidence in the man, a confidence he had not had when Orcutt had been merely the president of Inland Electronics. Edmund Orcutt had proved he could be depended upon to organize things and get them done. Devan was satisfied to think his smile meant he had the situation well in hand.

"Well, come on in," Orcutt said, advancing to them and extending his hand to Sudduth. "Glad to have you pay us a visit."

"Yeah," Sam said, following Orcutt's lead. "Sure glad you fellows could come up. How've you been, Blaine?" Sam shook hands heartily, though Blaine's hand was limp and his face expressionless.

Sudduth brushed off the familiarity. "You will send them out at once, please. We must be back by nightfall. Never can tell what you'll find in the woods."

"We've found nothing very ferocious," Orcutt said. "Except other human beings."

"Meaning what, mister?"

"Now, now, Orvid," Sudduth said. "Mr. Orcutt didn't mean anything by that, I'm sure."

"Where's Sister Abigail?" Devan asked. "Isn't she with you?"

"Almighty God has taken her, young man." Sudduth's face was grave.

"Pneumonia," Blaine complained.

"A wonderful woman, a gallant leader, a talented instrument of His grace, an instrument that was to help usher in the Golden Age except He had more use for her than I did."

"Amen," Blaine said.

"Now the deserters, please." Sudduth stood firm, his eye imperious, hands behind his back. A crowd was collecting at the gate.

Orcutt shook his head. "They came of their own free will, Eric. I'm afraid they'll have to leave the same way."

"You mean you're not going to bring them out, mister?"

"Be quiet, Orvid. I'll handle this."

"You have a death penalty for desertion. Why should they go to their deaths?"

"Oh, not really," Sudduth said. "That was just to scare them into staying. We need everybody we got."

"A wonderful way to run a group," Sam said.

"You can come in to get them if you like," Orcutt said. "That is, if you can talk them into going with you."

The nude men looked at each other, Sudduth with a crafty eye, Blaine with an angry one. They consented to go into the stockade.

Once inside, with the gate closed behind them, they became less of something out of the woods and more of something out of place within the enclosure. As they walked down the street with the others, they did so self-consciously, looking first this way and then that at the windows and doorways as if daring anyone to look askance at their nudity. They were rewarded by amused stares, giggles, oblique glances and outright laughter which surely must have unnerved them though they dared give no evidence of it. If it had been for these things alone, Sudduth might never have said anything. As it was, the barking dogs and the teasing children they belonged to brought Sudduth to a stop before they had gone more than a hundred paces.

"Do you have some clothes for us?" he asked. "It seems we're attracting considerable attention the way we are."

"You don't mind, do you?" Orcutt smiled. "Wouldn't wearing something be against His will, Eric? You've adhered so firmly to your convictions it wouldn't seem right somehow."

"In this instance I'm sure it wouldn't matter."

"I wish we had the clothes to give you, but we don't. It has been only recently we've been able to get enough skins to make a jacket and pants for each of us. Now, if you'd have waited until next week or maybe two weeks from now we could have given you something made out of cloth. We have a group on a project like that."

Orcutt sent the children away and the dogs followed. Then he drew out his clay pipe and leather bag of tobacco, proceeded to fill it. Sudduth followed his actions with envious eyes. Devan nearly laughed in his face because he remembered how much the man enjoyed his cigars; he was further amused because he knew there were plenty of extra clothes the two might have been given.

"Where'd you get the tobacco?"

"Oh, there's a patch of it not far from here."

"Where?"

"That would be telling, wouldn't it?" Orcutt lit his pipe with a match, drew long, ecstatic breaths on it. "Come along. You haven't seen the place."

"One moment."

"Yes, Eric?"

"Can you—has anyone thought of making cigars from the tobacco?"

"Of course. Why do you ask?" Orcutt blew a plume of smoke into the clear summer air.

"I smoked...before."

Orcutt studied him for a moment, then smiled. "How stupid of me. Of course you did. I should have remembered." He looked at Sam. "Do you have an extra cigar for our visitor, Sam?"

Sam drew out two cigars, gave one to Sudduth and put the other in his mouth when Blaine shook his head. He lit both of them. Sudduth inhaled with pleasant anticipation, suddenly went into a fit of coughing and when it was over he was red-eyed.

"Not used to it. I'll have to go easy." He took out the cigar, examined it with satisfaction. Then in surprise he jerked his head first to Sam, then to Orcutt. "You had *matches!*"

"Of course," Orcutt said. "What did you think they were?"

"Where did you get them? Who went back through the Needle?"

"Don't be a fool," Devan said. "We made them."

"How?"

"Phosphorus, wax, glue and little sticks."

"Hah!" Sudduth was triumphant. "Think I don't know anything, eh? I had high school chemistry, see? I know phosphorus. You can't just find it anywhere. You show me where it is." He turned to Blaine. "I've got them now. They can't get out of that."

Blaine grinned.

"It's all around you, this phosphorus," Devan said.

"You expect me to believe that?"

"You makin' a fool of him, mister?"

"No, Blaine."

"Come on, come on," Sudduth said smugly, his hands behind his back, his cigar in his mouth, rocking on the balls of his feet. "I'm waiting for an explanation."

"Well, you asked for it." Devan hurriedly reviewed the process, made sure he had it right. "You take animal bones and burn them. The ash that remains consists of nearly pure calcium phosphate. You heat this with sand and coke and the distillate is phosphorus."

"Simple, isn't it?" Orcutt said.

"You have to show me." But Sudduth sounded as if he'd been shown.

"We were planning to. Come on."

They walked along, passing the pottery shop, the glass project where Glenn Basher was busy and couldn't come out but waved at them, the brick factory, Orcutt all the while explaining everything to the two.

"That building there," Sudduth said. "You didn't say anything about it and it doesn't look like a dwelling."

They had passed a small, brick building with no skins over the windows. A peculiar smell emanated from it, a smell familiar to Devan, but one he was sure would not be familiar to Eric Sudduth. A small spiral of smoke rose from the chimney.

"It's the beverage department," Orcutt said. "Dr. Costigan is in charge. Wine and alcohol division."

"Interesting," Blaine said simply because Sudduth had been saying it to everything.

"It definitely is not interesting," Sudduth said vehemently. "Alcohol is the enemy of man, the despoiler of his body, the wrecker of his mind."

"Dr. Costigan would disagree with you," Sam Otto said. "And so would I."

"It's your privilege to hold that view, Eric," Orcutt said. "But what about doctors?"

"When there *are* doctors."

"We have two doctors here."

"Two doctors here?" The big man gazed at him disbelievingly, seemed to be digesting the information, then said sharply, "You were to lead us to the six, Mr. Orcutt."

Orcutt continued the circuitous tour showing them the paper manufacturing area, the felting unit, the match works, the spinners utilizing flax and a little cotton that had been found, and the carpentry shop.

"Hey!" Sudduth exclaimed when he saw a man at work there. "He's got a *hammer!*"

"Of course," Devan said. "I made it for him."

"You made it?"

"We have a smelting works," Orcutt explained. "You haven't seen that yet. We make tools out of steel. We're expanding every day."

Sudduth shook his head. "If the good Lord intended us to have these things, He'd have let them come along with us."

"He let us bring along our heads," Orcutt said. "That's where we kept the process of making steel until we needed it. So, using what else we have in our heads, we're going to make a loom and turn out a suit of clothes for everyone. There's a woman here who used to do weaving, swears she can turn out a suit a day and can't wait to get started. There are plenty of dressmakers among the women; they can double as tailors. We're going to set up a chemical laboratory, too. We have a young chemist who knows something about that; he's going to work in plastics. We're going to try to be as modern as we were before we came here."

"Hah!" Sudduth snorted. "You're going to bring the wrath of God down on us all by trying to duplicate the terrible things we had in the world we left behind."

"Amen," Blaine said.

"We're doing it better," Devan said. "We're not going to make the mistakes our fathers did. I can give you examples. First, the Indians used to put their meat between the leaves of the pawpaw tree and the white man thought it was just a ritual until he discovered why. There was something in the leaves that tenderized the meat. We know that now. A few years ago the vegetable enzyme from this tree was extracted and became popular as a meat tenderizer. Why can't we do that here? We have the advantage of all the past, you see.

"Second, take a look at monosodium glutamate, that salt that makes all our food taste better. We used to be so stupid we threw it away when we made beet sugar. It was just a useless by-product, we thought, until we learned better. We can have that here, too. Why not? Oh, we've found some things different—rabbits with long tails and squirrels that are white and six-pointed spring beauties—but basically everything's just about the same. We are ahead of the game already. We can make this place just about what we want it to be."

"*Yes*, Mr. Traylor. I agree with you. We can make it either godly or ungodly. We can do what you want or we can do what ought to be done. Take your choice."

"Amen," Blaine said.

"Nuts," Devan said.

"Amen," Sam said.

When they had finished their inspection of the camp, Orcutt led them to the biggest building of the settlement, the assembly hall. It was a plain structure with brick sides and a ceiling of chinked logs covered with grass.

"What's this place?" Sudduth asked, walking across the ground past the front benches to the table in the middle of one end of the building.

"Our courthouse, meeting place, dance hall," Orcutt said.

"*Dance* hall?" Sudduth said as if he hated the words.

"Square dancing mostly, Eric. Ever tried it? It's fun. Some of the kids are working up an orchestra for regular dancing. Won't you sit down?" He indicated the first row bench. "You know Mr. Tooksberry, don't you?" He gestured to a man at another table a little farther away. "He's writing our constitution and by-laws. We're going to have a convention before long to adopt them. Mr. Tooksberry used to be a lawyer with Inland before his displacement. He remembers the statutes rather well. Because he knew something of the law, he performed the wedding ceremonies for those who wanted to get married."

Tooksberry was writing laboriously with a quill. "I'd give anything for a pen. Even a ball-point. It's hard enough writing without my glasses."

"Where's your secretary?" Devan asked. To Sudduth he said, "You remember Miss Beatrice Treat? She's his wife and secretary now."

"Left for obvious reasons a few moments before you people came in." Tooksberry smiled at them, made a gesture that included all the papers on the table. "My big opportunity. I can include all the laws I thought were good, forget all the bad ones. A tremendous responsibility, I'll tell you. Of course many of the laws I knew will not be applicable, such as traffic laws. But then the statutes we adopt can always be revised in such an eventuality."

"All very enlightening," Sudduth said with disgust. "Will you please bring in the six I'm to take back with me, Mr. Orcutt?"

"You mean if they agree to go with you."

A boy of about sixteen years of age came into the hall. "Mr. Orcutt, sir," he said, "those people wouldn't come. They said they didn't want to see either Mr. Sudduth or Mr. Blaine."

"All right," Orcutt said. The boy ran out. "There's your answer, Eric."

"You think you can fool me like that?" Sudduth said, his face darkening. "It's obvious you told the boy to say that."

"You're wrong. He was telling the truth. I could have told you that before, only I wanted you to hear it yourself. It took so long to contact all six persons because they all are working in different places. All except one that I know had a dental appointment."

"Dental appointment?" Sudduth's eyebrows rose slowly, his face became calmer and his eyes lost their fire. "Did you say *dental* appointment?" When Orcutt nodded, he added, "That means you have a dentist here."

"A logical conclusion," Orcutt said, laughing a little. "Do you mean to tell me you didn't know that? A Dr. Van Ness. Didn't you meet him before?"

"He's very good, too," Devan said.

"You knew that everyone lost his fillings during the transition, didn't you?"

"Of course. We've been using clay and beeswax and sap. What kind of treatment does this Van Ness give?"

"He uses gold," Devan said. "I've had several filled. See?" He displayed teeth into which Dr. Van Ness had laboriously pounded gold with a mallet.

"Beautiful job." Sudduth was impressed. He sighed. "He's a good dentist."

"The best," Sam said.

"I got bad teeth," Blaine said.

"So have the people back in your caves," Devan said. "It's a pity they can't have theirs fixed up."

Eric Sudduth was wringing his hands.

"Too bad the fillings will drop out when we go through the Needle again," Orcutt said.

"Through the Needle again?" Sudduth eyed him wonderingly. "When are we going to do that and how?"

"When we get the second Needle built."

The silence was suddenly oppressive inside the building. From far off came sounds of activity, children's cries, the clink of metal, the clang of hammer on metal. A bee that wandered inside zoomed around the men for a few moments and then, as if sensitive to the tension there, zoomed out again.

Eric Sudduth's lips were thin, his forehead corrugated as he stood there shaking his head. "I forbid it!"

"It's the only way we'll ever get back," Devan said gently. "We've got to make another Needle."

"You can't do it!" Sudduth shouted, his eyes round, his face white with rage. "Look what happened when you made the last one against my advice. God's wrath leveled against all of you connected with the Needle and your needless experimentation has resulted in this. Our not putting on garments is our penance for evil ways and you should do the same. This is your hell, don't you see? And mine, too, because I didn't stop you."

"You sent Orvid Blaine," Orcutt said. "He nearly did."

"He failed and you wouldn't listen." Sudduth was grave. "We must now be penitent. You can't make another Needle. We mustn't let you. The punishment God would impose on us all if we broke His laws a second time would be horrible."

"Where do you get the idea this is all against God's wishes, anyway?" Devan asked.

"Isn't it obvious? Can't you see it all around you? Are you all so stupid you won't believe your eyes? This place this time. Where will it be next time?"

"You'd better quiet down," Orcutt said.

"Nobody tells Mr. Sudduth to be quiet, mister."

"Shut up, Orvid," Sudduth said. "Come on, we're leaving. You can keep the six. I refuse to have anything to do with people who can't see God's handwriting on the wall."

"Amen," Blaine said.

15

It was early October before Devan got his share of glass for his cottage windows. It wasn't so bad being without it during the day but the nights had been rather chilly and he wasted no time getting the panes in place because, if this Northern Illinois was like the other Northern Illinois, there was plenty of precedent for chill winds and cold rains even in the daytime. There was no sense in taking a chance of getting the inside of the cottage wet.

As it was, it was a Sunday afternoon when Devan received word his glass was ready and, since Betty was home, too, they both went to Basher's glass shop to pick it up. Even at that they were among the last in the camp to get glass because, for one thing, Devan didn't want to take advantage of his position and friendship with Orcutt to get it and, for another, there were other families whose need was greater: families with babies and children, elderly people, sick people, though there were few of the latter. It was remarkable, Devan reflected, that as busy as they all had been there had been no ill people to speak of, though a hospital had been one of the first buildings to be constructed in the stockade. And of course it and other public buildings had been enclosed in glass first, too.

The first glass was brittle, green and almost opaque and Basher had had a time trying to improve it until the old storekeeper, Elmo Hodge, the amateur astronomer, heard about it and told Basher how to correct the tint by adding chemicals which would create a complementary color and the unwanted hues would cancel each other out. He knew about it because of his work with telescopes, which brought him into contact with lenses and optics. He got interested in the process and was working alongside Basher making just plain glass for windows and planning the manufacture of lenses for telescopes, binoculars and microscopes, though plans for the last-mentioned items had not as yet been perfected.

"If I remember right," Hodge said, "you have to replace the potassium to get hard glass, replace some of the calcium with lead to get the flint glass you can make lenses out of." He rubbed his hands together. "After that we can concentrate on plate glass, safety glass, Pyrex and coated lenses. It will take time but it will be worth it." Devan had heard those words a lot lately, had heard himself say them many times.

The glass he and Betty carried to their cottage had only a trace of green and it was quite clear. The windows had been made with what the camp had adopted as a module. A man who was known to have been exactly six feet tall served as the basis for the module and inches were arrived at by the proper division of his length, down to the inch. Since the window sash had been made only a fraction of an inch larger than the glass, the pane fitted in very nicely, though Devan took the precaution of bedding it in with putty someone in the camp had made from linseed oil and limestone.

Betty insisted on helping, so they worked together, Devan spreading a thin layer of putty on the wood prior to Betty's pressing the glass into the sash and securing it firmly with glazier's points of Devan's own manufacture. Then she added the outside putty.

When he finished his last window, Betty had only half finished her part of the job. Not because she was slower. She simply had more to do. So he came around the cottage to where she was working in the warm afternoon sun, being careful not to step in flower beds she had taken time to plant. He came up to her and stopped to watch her work.

"You the foreman?" she asked.

"Damn right. You on a slow-down?"

"Until I get a raise in pay, yes."

"You're overpaid now."

"You can take over the job any time you want."

"Carry on."

She flashed white teeth at him and continued. Betty was still the same woman he had known back at the Rasmussen factory. She had lost none of the intense look in her dark blue eyes and, though she had done a man's work in the stockade from orderly in the hospital to helping on the sewing and weaving projects, she had lost none of her grace. The errant forelock still fell over her eye now and then and her black hair was soft and wavy as it fell to her shoulders. She was brown of arm, suntanned of face and her long legs were nicely bronzed. He decided there was no one in New Chicago quite as attractive.

She gave him a look. "What's the great thought?"

"Just thinking about you."

"You didn't have to say that."

"I wouldn't have, if it weren't true."

She smiled again as if it were something beautiful inside that caused her lips to part and her eyes to brighten.

He had to kiss her.

"Is it wrong, Dev?" She held him away and looked at him.

"Is what wrong?" He knew what she meant. When she didn't answer, he said softly, "I don't think so."

Both had had children before and they missed them and felt it not fair to talk about them since they avoided all talk about their former families. When they did mention children, they did so casually, generally and evasively. Now they had reason to talk about them openly, specifically.

There was a commotion to their left down the long way designated as Orcutt Street that ran clear to the gate, a gate they had worked feverishly to make in the early days and which now was left open all the time because there was nothing to close it against.

"Somebody's yelling outside," Betty said. "People are running out."

Things happened so seldom in New Chicago they found themselves walking excitedly to the gate and through it. There was a crowd around something on the ground. When they got close enough, Devan and

Betty could see that it was a nude man on a stretcher made of twined reeds and two stout branches. The man was Eric Sudduth and he was in pain. His face was paler than Devan had ever seen it before. His breath was rapid, sweat making his body shine. He rolled his eyes.

"Give me a hand," Devan said, reaching for one end of one of the branches. "Let's get him to the hospital."

"Let me alone," Sudduth groaned, twisting a little on the reeds. "Let me die. God wants me to die."

The stretcher-bearers met Orcutt on the way to the hospital. "What's going on?" he asked. Then he saw the man on the reeds.

"They brought him up to the gate and left him," Devan said.

"Let me die," Sudduth said. He turned to Orcutt. "Make them let me die."

In the hospital Sudduth's sickness was quickly diagnosed as appendicitis and he was rushed into the operating room. Orcutt asked Devan to stay with the man temporarily and act in his behalf and Betty, saying she had nothing better to do, stayed with him.

"You know how Eric dislikes Dr. Costigan and alcohol," Devan said when he and Betty were waiting for the man to come back from the operating room. "Just think: he's being anesthetized with ether made by Renthaler from grain alcohol distilled by Dr. Costigan."

"I don't think you'd better tell him."

"He's being operated on with a scalpel made out of carbon steel manufactured and sharpened to a razor edge by Gus Nelson, who likes to drink. He's being stitched with catgut through the courtesy of that old mountain goat who ate too many grape pulps and we had to butcher."

"One thing I do know," Betty said. "He couldn't be operated on by two surer, more confident men than the two who are doing the job."

"They were interns just seven months ago. Interns at Cook County Hospital, wondering where and how they were to start their practices. Now the health of all of New Chicago depends on them."

They were both at Sudduth's side that night when he came out of the ether and when he finally quit his thrashing around on the hospital cot and regained consciousness. He looked up with bloodshot eyes and said hoarsely, "Go away," sending ether breath their way. He retched. Betty was practically professional.

"Don't talk if you don't want to," Devan said. "We won't bother you."

It was eerie, then, the three of them there in the flickering candlelight in the rustic room, Sudduth lying like a corpse, looking up at the log ceiling, his eyes puffy, his face ashen, his lips cracked, Devan and Betty sitting silent in chairs near by. Only occasionally would Sudduth blink his eyes.

"I'm not staying," Sudduth said, finally.

"You'll stay the required number of days," Devan said.

"Who are you, the doctor?"

"Guess again."

"How long do I have to stay?"

"About a week in bed."

"It's twenty miles to your camp, Eric," Betty said. "You couldn't expect to walk there for several weeks."

Sudduth snorted. "Orvid Blaine brought me here. Had those stupid men carry me all the way. I could wring his neck. God wanted me to die. Wasn't that plain to him? Couldn't he feel it in his bones as I could in mine? Why didn't you let me die?"

"If God wanted you to die," Devan said, "He'd have made the doctor's hand less skillful while you were on the operating table."

"You brought me in here, so I'm not beholden to you or anybody in this camp. I didn't want an operation."

"Maybe it would have been a good idea to let you die. At least we wouldn't have an ungrateful man on our hands."

"Griping comes natural to Eric," Betty said. "That only shows he's getting back to normal."

The convalescence of Eric Sudduth was something to behold. From the first meal his cheeks lost their paleness, became ruddy. His lusterless eyes grew brighter and his disposition kept pace. Betty found it easy to convince him that, since he was going to be in the hospital for a while, he might as well have the gold fillings his teeth needed. This pleased him.

Devan liked to think the person responsible for the change in the man was Betty, for she had asked to be assigned to him, stating that all Sudduth needed was a little love. She saw that he got it. She had everybody in the camp visiting him and bringing him things to eat and listening to his ideas. He took to the easy chairs in the sunroom the first days in November, enjoyed sitting there smoking long cigars, his hospital robe barely able to cover his paunch, talking with the people who came to see him, conversing with Betty when there was no one else around. He looked content.

The second week in November was not as good, Betty reported.

"Eric's glancing at people sort of sideways," she said. "He's not sleeping too well, the nurse says."

The third week he made his announcement.

"Eric wants to go back to his people. I wish you'd go talk to him, Dev. I've done all I can."

Devan found him in the sunroom looking a little disgruntled.

"It's my bounden duty," he told Devan after the sparring was over. "God would have me with my people and that's where I'm going."

"That isn't the kind of life for you," Devan said. "A man like you just getting over an operation. You still need care."

"I'm as sound as a dollar," Sudduth said, pounding his chest with his fist and then, embarrassed, finding he had to cough. "Well, I am anyway."

"It's getting mighty cold out. Are you sure you want to go?"

"My personal wishes are of no account. It's my devotion to duty. That's all I have to think about." He looked out the windows, saw the leaves letting go and falling to the earth, dipped the end of his cigar in his ashtray. "God will give me the strength."

"You're going to need it."

"I'm leaving tomorrow. Told the doctors. Told the nurse."

"What do they say?"

"It doesn't matter."

Devan came to the hospital to see him off the next day, gave him a box of cigars.

"I'll walk to the gate with you," Devan said.

"Kind of you."

They started out on a cool, wet and windy November lead-sky day, both bent against the wind, coats flapping in the breeze.

When they came to the gate, Sudduth handed Devan the coat and Devan was shocked to see the man had nothing on underneath.

"Don't be a damned fool!" Devan said. "You'll freeze to death without anything on!"

"If my people can do it, so can I," he said, drawing himself to his full height. "You don't hear them complaining, do you?" He turned and strode away, a ludicrous figure of a man, box of cigars under one arm, gingerly walking barefoot over the ground.

Devan knew the man could not make it; it was only a question of how long he would last. He figured he'd wait at the gate and if he didn't come back soon, he'd get somebody and they'd go look for him.

He didn't have to get anybody.

In a few minutes Sudduth came limping into sight, his box of cigars still under his arm, his hands clutching his right side.

"I—I'm not used to walking, I guess," Sudduth said, his lips blue, hands white, skin goosefleshed and teeth chattering. "I've got a pain in my side. I guess I'm not ready to try it yet."

"You'll probably get pneumonia."

"Let me have my coat."

Devan handed him his coat and they walked back to the hospital where Devan sat him in front of the fire in the sunroom and got something hot for him to drink. The man shivered for a long time, finally took his hands away from his side, gave a sigh.

"My box, please," he said, indicating the box of cigars on the table. "I need a cigar."

Part Three: Decision

16

The three children ran chasing each other down the beach, their bare feet kicking up a shower of spray when they veered into the small waves and then back again, this way and that, in the waves and out, reversing, getting their clothes wet, the girl in the lead and the two smaller children, the boys, giving her a hard chase. They shrieked and screamed and their laughter and cries floated out over the lake while the sands of the shore recorded their footprints in a profusion that would deny analysis.

Finally, they tired and walked back to the grass at the rise and fell exhausted to the ground there, all of them breathing as if they were the last breaths they would ever take and laughing even as they did this.

"I'm run out," Don said, panting. "You should have let us catch you, Sally, and then we wouldn't have run so much."

"I wish Don and me could fly," Ralph said. "We'd sure catch you then, wouldn't we, Don?"

"She didn't get in the water. Girls can't swim good."

"I can so," Sally said. "I could swim right now."

"Don't you let Daddy catch you, Sal," Ralph said.

"Would you be an old tattletale if I did?"

"I dare you," Don said. "Double dare you."

"Donny Tooksberry, you know better than that."

"'Fraidy cat," Ralph said.

"You be quiet, Ralph. Both of you be quiet and I'll tell you a story."

"What kind of a story?"

"One about what's out there?" Don's arm indicated the entire horizon.

"I want to hear something new, Sal. I heard all about the Needle and how Daddy met Mommy on the other side and how—"

"Let *her* tell it."

"I wasn't going to tell about that," Sally said.

"It's not true anyway. It's a fairy story."

Sally turned to Ralph and looked him in the eyes. "Ralph, how dare you say a thing like that? You know very well it's true. Would Mommy and Daddy lie to us?"

"Heck, you really believe that stuff, Sal?"

"You saying you don't believe it either?"

"Shucks." Don dug his fingers in the grass and sand and brought some sand up and let it fall through his fingers. "It's bad to say it, but"—he looked up and saw encouragement in her eyes—"but how can you believe about the buildings they tell about?"

"My father is an *engineer*," Sally said. "An engineer is a thing you study for. You go to a school and study for years and years. And when you are done you know how to build buildings like that or—or a Needle like Daddy's building right now."

"I heard Mom tell Sal about it, Donny."

Don curled his lips. "You ever seen a building like what they talk about?"

"I don't have to," Sally said. "And that's not all. What about automobiles and television and phonographs and ice cream sodas? You've seen pictures of those drawn by the artists and hanging in the art museum."

"I learned that stuff in school."

"You learned other things, too, Don."

Don smiled. "I was only teasing."

Sally was lying on the grass, her shoulders supported by elbows, her eyes looking far out at the horizon. "It's right out there somewhere that we came from, they say."

"I'd give anything to see an airplane," Don said. "Just one. A teeny-weeny one even."

"What about a jet?" Ralph said. He made a jet noise, played his hands were the plane.

"The movies, they say, were grand," Sally said.

"Oh, we'll have all that stuff some day," Don said.

"When we get back?"

"We're going back," Ralph said. "My Daddy said so."

All three looked out over the blue water.

"Let's all be together when we do," Don said. "Let's never be apart ever."

"I'm going to want a ride in an airplane. A jet. First thing. They were working on rockets, Daddy said. Maybe I could ride one of them."

"I wonder," Sally said, her chin in her hands. "I wonder what it's really like back there."

Don stood up, shaded his eyes with his hand.

"What are you doing?" Sally asked.

"Looking."

Sally looked too. "I don't see anything."

"Down there." Don pointed to a spot at the water's edge.

"What's down there?" Ralph asked, a little frightened and coming close to them.

"What is it?"

"Let's go down and see."

"No," Ralph yelled. "Don't go down there."

"Aw, come on," Don said. "We'll take care of you."

They walked down the slope to the beach and then down the beach to a place where a small, furry object lay in the waves.

Don went over, kicked it out of the water.

"It's a rabbit," Ralph said, all the excitement going out of him.

"Yeah," Don said.

"Wait a minute," Sally said, examining the rabbit closely. "Notice anything strange about this rabbit?"

Don looked for a moment. "Somebody cut his tail off."

"A funny rabbit," Ralph said. "No tail."

Sally's blue eyes were puzzled. "No, it's not that it was cut off. It looks like it grew into that little ball of fur instead of long and slim like it's supposed to be."

"How could it grow into a ball?"

"I don't know."

"Well, if you don't, then I don't either. Let's play tag again." Don hit her arm with his hand. "You're it, Sal."

"I'm not playing, Donny." She took Ralph's hand. "We're going home."

The three took one last look at the rabbit.

"Are the children home yet?" Devan closed the screen door, put the folio of the New Chicago *News* on a table and kissed Betty before he sank into his easy chair and lit a cigarette.

"I thought you were they," Betty said, glancing out the window.

"They've been gone most of the afternoon. Don Tooksberry came by. They went down to the beach. Any news?"

Devan reached for the newspaper and unfolded it. He scanned the headlines. "Nothing startling. I didn't see them from the Needle building. But then I was pretty busy."

"Think you'll be ready for the test tomorrow night?"

"We're ready right now. Final adjustments tonight."

Concern crossed her face like a fleeting shadow and Betty turned away, starting for the kitchen. Devan watched her go, knew what she was thinking.

"Remember the last time?" she called from the kitchen.

Devan sighed. How could he forget how Basher had gone through *Needle I* even if it was ten years ago? And then thinking about it flooded his mind with associated recollections, including how Mrs. Basher had not believed that her husband had gone through the Eye and how she had gone to the police. Had they ever told Glenn about that?

"The way it happened last time," Betty said, "you all drew straws and the winner was really the loser, for a time anyway. Is that going to happen again?"

"Can't happen again. At least the person who goes through won't fall in a lake."

"How do you know for sure, Dev?"

"You remember the little Needle we made, don't you?"

"The one you can only put your hand through?"

"That's it. If we had had any sense on the other side, we'd have used the little one. Then we wouldn't have got into the trouble we did. If you call this trouble." Devan put his cigarette out, went to the kitchen and mixed a drink while Betty continued dinner. "As it is, Dr. Costigan made a small model here first, too, and we started with that, trying to put an arm through and finding it wouldn't go."

"Why not?"

"Didn't I tell you?"

"If you did, I forgot."

"We couldn't put a hand through it because we were stopped by something solid. Wouldn't go into the Eye at all. Then we knew we were underground on the other side of the Eye. We moved the Needle a little at a time up the hill toward the lake, moving the electrical equipment right along with us. Took us some time. But we finally got to the top of that knoll and there the hand and arm went through and could feel ground a foot below. So, you see? It can't happen again. When you go through *Needle II* you know you're not going to fall into a lake. You can walk through and back again."

Betty smiled. "You're a trusting soul, I swear, Devan."

"Why do you say that?" He was a bit annoyed.

"Nobody's gone through it yet, still you're perfectly confident everything's going to be all right."

"We've been working on it for ten years and this time we've taken everything into consideration and won't make any silly mistakes."

"Will you answer me one question, then?"

He tossed off the last of his drink. "What's that?"

"How do you know you're back in Chicago when you walk through it?"

Devan colored slightly and fought for control. She had touched a vital point, it was true, one that had been discussed considerably, but it wouldn't do to worry her about it or to let her think any of them weren't confident....

"I must have come close," she teased. "Your face shows it."

"It's just that I'm ashamed my wife, of all people, doesn't know all the facts. Here I've been in charge of the thing all these years and you've forgotten how that part was to be managed."

"Tell me, then."

"Reversed polarity. Just like an electric motor. You reverse the polarity and it runs the other way. On the second Needle we're running the current through the opposite way to create the opposite conditions. Didn't I ever tell you these things?"

"You have, Dev. I guess I forgot. But this time I want you to be sure of what you're doing."

He studied her face. "Why are you so concerned so suddenly?"

"Suddenly? I wasn't taken with this idea just a moment ago. I've been thinking about it for a long time."

He had never seen Betty like this. "For heaven's sake, tell me what this is all about!"

"Really, there's nothing to tell, Dev. What I meant was that I've been worried about the second Needle and what it will mean. You know we didn't have much choice about coming here and we want to be able to decide about the next transition, don't we?"

"We won't be caught unawares," Devan said, still worried about the look in her eyes and unconvinced by her explanation. "There aren't any more Sudduthites to throw pipes into the machinery."

"Not unless Eric gets a bee in his bonnet again."

"He won't do that. He's too interested in trying to recreate the whole Bible. That man has a fantastic faculty for remembering Bible verses."

Dinner hour lacking only the children, Betty put the food in the oven and they moved to the chairs in front of the house.

"You know, Dev," Betty said, lighting a cigarette and exhaling a ribbon of smoke, "the Sudduthites didn't turn out to be so bad, did they?"

"Not after they got here and were absorbed. Just think of how many we know, Betty. Even the two from that night on the beach. Funny what people will do under stress, when the controls are off."

Betty laughed. "Some of the women are in my clubs. To look at them you'd never think they once chose to live naked in caves."

"Once they got back with us, things moved forward again, not backward as they did in the caves. We got some good workers out of the bunch."

They sat quietly now in the later afternoon sunlight, the sound of their neighbors coming to them across the yards. Somewhere someone was using the lawn mower — they had allowed only one to be made. After all, it could be rotated, used by everyone easily enough; besides technical help was at a premium, particularly mechanical help.

They could hear voices raised in argument and they looked at each other and smiled. The Bradleys were at it again. Was this, Devan thought, so different from Chicago's West Side or Chicago's any side? How many times he had said that to himself! Yet he knew that, as people, there would have to be changes in them, subtle changes that had come with the passing of the years and the living in the wilderness, changes that he was not aware of but that he was certain were there.

Yes, it would be quite a shock to get back to the old ways, to the old scenes, the old people. An unpleasant shock, really. And the thought of going back, the memory of the old gray buildings, the back yards viewed from the elevated trains, the dirty water of the Chicago River, the littered paper in Grant Park on a Monday morning, people pushing and shoving, door-to-door salesmen, the smoke-filled air, the lack of recognition in any eye — all this made the prospect uninviting. But he had always disliked city life, the confinement it necessitated, the habits it made one acquire. Then why go back? This thought was startling but easily answered. Because everyone was going back, if the Needle worked, and there wouldn't be anyone left. Yes, he'd have to go back.

He saw the children coming down the roadway and his heart gave a thump of excitement when he did because he loved them so. He seemed to have more time for his children on this side of the Eye.

"Daddy!" Sally said, running up to him and throwing her arms around him. "Donny says there isn't any 'back there.' Tell me there is, please, Daddy."

"Why, of course there is, darling. Donny's never been there. But your mother and I have."

"Are there real big buildings there like you say, Daddy?" Ralph wanted to know. And when Devan said there were, he asked, "Why did they build them so big?"

"So that all the people will have places to work."

"But couldn't the people work outside the building?" Sally was the curious one now.

Devan looked at Betty, who said, "You're the quizmaster tonight, Mr. Traylor. Go ahead and answer her."

"Well." Devan cleared his throat. This was a stickler. Why *did* they build them so high? "You see, Sally, so many people live in such a small area, if they were all spread out with a space for each one to work in, it would take many square miles. So they have office buildings that reach up into the sky and give them spaces one on top of the other so they don't have to go so far to work or to get home."

"But what kind of work could there be to do off the ground?"

"Oh, paper work, idea work, planning and working out schedules and balancing books; there are a lot of things they do."

"How do they get up to the top?"

"Elevator. You know that."

Devan turned to Ralph who had been tugging at his pants leg. "How many people live in Chicago?" Ralph asked.

"Millions. Three or four million, I think."

"*Millions!*" Sally was dumbfounded. "Do they *all* work in big buildings?"

"Now, Sally!" Betty said. "Surely you learned about things like that in school, didn't you?"

"Well, not exactly those things. We learned about airplanes and automobiles and Indians. Will there be real Indians there when we get there?"

"Only on reservations."

"You know?" Sally said. "I think I'd like to go there on a visit. But I think I'd like to live here better. There wouldn't be room for us there, would there?"

"A jet plane makes a big *whoosh!*" Ralph said. "Will I ever get to see a jet plane, Daddy?"

"What's a department store, Daddy?"

"How does a merry-go-round work?"

"You might ask your father what a night club is, where the Chicago Cubs are this season and whether or not he's a bull or a bear on the stock market. He'd be glad to explain, I'm sure."

17

Devan walked down the stone path, a pleasant summer night's breeze coming in off the lake, his step brisk, his spirits bright. He saw the tower of *Needle II,* a shaft of metal that rose from the top of the wooden building beneath and as he looked at it he thought: You are what ten years of my life look like, ten years that I don't know the value of because I don't know if you'll work.

But tomorrow we'll know the truth.

He laughed when he thought of how they all had at first thought it would be a matter of a few years—five at the most. And it *had* looked easy. But the big generators had been the stumbling block after the steam engines had been built. Still later there were some metals they couldn't find, some methods they had forgotten, some processes no person in New Chicago had remembered. They had to be ingenious about these things, substituting some items and bypassing others.

It had looked sometimes as if the Needle would never be built, but there it was on the sandy knoll overlooking the lake, a black shaft against a sky full of stars. Would it be worth all the trouble? And, most important of all, would it take them back to Chicago? Tomorrow was the night, even though it would probably be ready for the test in a few hours. The very thought made his heart give a flip-flop. Why not have a preview tonight?

He put down the feeling, reflecting that it would not be exactly cricket. *Needle II* was New Chicago's single objective, the result of Orcutt's driving power through the months and years. To go through in advance of his knowing would be taking advantage of him. There were others to think of, too; everyone in New Chicago had a share in *Needle II.*

"That damned Needle!" How many times had people said that in the past ten years! It had become familiar when wire that might have expanded the telephone circuits and had taken a year to make was suddenly requisitioned for new windings in the Needle, when tubes that might have gone into a radio system were made solely for circuits in the Needle, when men who might have worked on engines, refrigerators, deep freezes, garbage-disposal units, manufactured gas and hundreds of other things were asked to work on some phase of construction for the Needle instead.

There were still problems, though they were different now. For example, what would happen in Chicago when people started popping out of nowhere with no clothes on? How would people go through? What kind of a system would they work out for the transition?

He walked up the wooden steps to the door and stepped through to the inside of the *Needle II* room. Electric lights—how hard the bulbs had been to make!—illuminated a room far different from the big room inside the Rasmussen Stove Company building. This one had a ceiling only eight feet high and encompassed a Needle much smaller than the one that had brought them there. *Needle II* was only four feet in diameter and the Eye barely gave a man enough room to crawl into. The Needle was only twenty feet high and the Eye was correspondingly smaller, a foot and a half wide by two and one-half feet high. Small as it was, it was still big enough for any New Chicagoan to go through, though he'd have to inch his way through on his side.

The Needle pointed at the sky out the roof of a building only fifteen feet square. Absent were the neat cabinets and panels of the first Needle. They were luxuries here where there were only bare necessities. The circuits and tubes and other electronic devices accessory to the Needle were arrayed on a number of breadboards and scattered over the floor and on the walls in profusion. Electricity to work it all came from New Chicago's power plant just outside the stockade.

Dr. Costigan was at work on the wiring behind one of the panels he had removed from the shaft.

"Working yet?" Devan sat on a stool, watched the doctor handle the wires that led to one of the important circuit boxes only he knew the function of. The doctor, after all the years, had insisted on keeping his secret, and they had not tried to pry it out of him. Devan had provided him with all the materials he needed and knew the circuits almost as well as the doctor. Still he did not know how the key boxes worked, but he respected the old man's penchant for security.

"I've gone over all the circuits. They've all checked out but this one. Just a loose connection, I think."

Dr. Costigan looked pretty much as he had ten years before, Devan decided as he watched him work over the circuit with a test light. This was rather surprising considering the fact that Devan had judged him to be in his sixties even then. He was just as tall, maybe a little stockier, but with the same stoop, the same watery blue eyes and the same unquenchable thirst.

"Think we could get it to work tonight?"

The doctor turned around slowly. "Sure. The big test is tomorrow night, though. But if you like, we can make a routine check."

"Don't you think we've made enough routine checks? With the little Needle, I mean. We know, for example, that it's no warmer or cooler on the other side, that the surface is hard, though a little yielding."

"I know. Maybe it's somebody's living room carpet. Or the asphalt of a street." The doctor turned back. "Could be the back yard lot where the kids play baseball. We'll find out tomorrow night."

"We could find out tonight."

The doctor spun around, looked at Devan in surprise. "Who could find out? Who would go through?"

"Oh, I might go through."

"You?" The doctor's mouth dropped open. "Why, you couldn't do that, Devan!"

Devan laughed. "I know. But I've been thinking about it." He looked at the Eye illuminated now from both sides, looking much smaller but its polished metal sides looking just as efficient as the other Eye. At least you can't fall into this one, he thought. When the people go through they'll have to work their way into it.

"I've been thinking, too," the doctor said soberly. "I didn't want to mention it, but we haven't even made the rabbit test this time. Just shoved our hands in. I wonder if that's enough. Of course I've got too many fillings in my old teeth to go putting my head in there."

Devan lit a cigarette and came over to where the doctor was. "I wonder if it goes through to Chicago? Suppose it's not Chicago but some place like this? Or something even more different?"

"It's a possibility," the doctor said. "I'm not denying that."

"Don't you wonder about it?"

"Don't twist my arm too much or I'll turn it on and have a look."

Devan's heart was beating fast now. His will and the idea were having a battle inside. Was there really anything wrong with his going through at once? It would satisfy ten years of waiting one day sooner. The fact that he ought to wait that one more day was suddenly overbalanced by the fact that nothing would be actually accomplished by putting it off.

"Turn it on and I'll have a look," Devan said.

The doctor's head said no. "Your fillings. You'd lose them all again."

"So what? It will be all right. The big test is tomorrow night and we'll all lose ours then anyway, or soon after when we go back. So, when I come out I'll put wax in the cavities until after the big test. Then I can let them know I went through tonight."

The doctor chuckled. "Well, I guess it really doesn't make much difference which night we go through, does it?"

"Ten years' work and then waiting for twenty-four hours just because of a schedule. It doesn't make sense."

"We've talked ourselves into it, haven't we?"

"I'm ready when you are."

"You be careful, hear?" The doctor softened the admonition with a smile.

A half hour later Dr. Costigan pulled the master switch that set tubes to glowing and other devices to humming and clicking. He and Devan carefully checked important test points with a volt-ohmmeter, the doctor making a few confidential checks of his own.

Devan made a sweep of his hand through part of the Eye, noted with satisfaction that it vanished momentarily. "It's working all right."

"Are you sure you want to do this, Dev?" Dr. Costigan said, his voice edged with worry. "What if you don't come back?"

"I'll come back." He put his hand deep into the lower part of the Eye, felt the hard surface a foot below the opening. Then he sat at the edge of the Eye, his feet disappearing into it. He could feel the ground below. He looked up, waved at the doctor.

"Good luck," the doctor said.

Devan slid into the Eye.

He saw angry clouds that scudded across the sky in a world of stone outcropping and grass for as far as he could see. The moon rode high and bright, illuminating the rolling hills of rock, light patches chasing one another as the clouds hurried along.

It wasn't cold, but Devan shivered as the soughing air threatened to blow him from the spot.

This is not Chicago.

He had tried to prepare himself for it but in spite of it the realization hit him hard: This is not Chicago.... Repeating the words numbed him.

There wasn't a living thing in sight.

He bent down and touched the rock. It was hard, like igneous rock in a way, but it was different because it gave just a little. He dared not move from where he was because the Eye was right behind him and he wanted to be able to step back through it in a hurry, if he had to. If he wandered from it he'd never find it again in this monotonous world.

He yelled. His voice was lost on the breeze and nothing answered. He swore at the top of his lungs. Nothing, no one answered.

Not a thing stirred. Only the wind and the waving short-cropped grass that grew in the tiny crannies. This could not be any place in the world he knew.

Ten years' work gone. Now the whole thing would have to be redone or tried some other way. He and Dr. Costigan would have to decide how to change the Needle to make its Eye go back to Chicago.

He took one more look at the desolate place, then stepped backward. Dr. Costigan was there, expectant. The bright room was cheery.

"Well?" The doctor's eyes were curious.

"It's not Chicago," Devan said. "Just dreary, rocky country for as far as you can see. I don't think anything exists there. At least I didn't see anything."

The doctor looked at him for a long time before he pulled the master switch. "You'd better pick up your fillings."

Devan knelt and retrieved them, feeling the holes in his teeth with his tongue at the same time. When he had the last one in his pocket, the doctor handed him a glass.

"Let's drink," the doctor said. "Drink to commemorate what you probably consider ten years of working for nothing."

"I wouldn't say that," Devan said, letting the doctor fill his glass with wine. "We have the Needle to experiment with. We can try some other way."

The doctor shook his head gravely. "There is no other way."

Devan looked at him sharply. "No other way? What do you mean by that?"

"Just what I said. There's nothing we can do."

"We can reverse the polarity and see what happens. That's one thing."

"It wouldn't help."

"Why not?"

"I did it with *Needle I*," the doctor said, looking sheepishly into his half-empty glass. "I changed the polarity accidentally and it didn't make any difference because Glenn went through when it was one way and the detective went through when it was the other way. They both ended up here."

Devan suddenly needed another drink, poured it from the bottle. The doctor finished his own drink and refilled his glass.

"I didn't think we'd ever get back to Chicago, Devan. This is a continuous thing. You could keep going from one universe to another by means of a Needle, each universe just like the last and complete itself, yet each one deceptively different, as we've noticed here. I think we were lucky to end up on an earth as nice as this one."

"I suppose," Devan said, "if you kept going through enough universes you'd finally get back to the one you started from."

"It's a guess, but I'd say you'd have to go through an infinite number of them."

Devan finished his drink and put the glass down. "You couldn't even make a Needle in the world on the other side of this Eye. Unless you made it out of grass and rock."

"I'm just an old experimenter," the doctor mused, sloshing the wine around in the bottom of his glass and watching it. "That's what everybody thinks, anyway. That very first night I knew we all needed a goal, an incentive to keep us together. I saw Orcutt give us organization. I furnished the motive that stuck it together. The Needle and eventual return. It was simple to say, 'Just reverse the polarity and we'll get back all right.' But I didn't think we'd really get back. Not even then."

"I'll be damned."

"Have another drink," the doctor said, reaching for his glass. "Living with the thought for ten years and

not telling anyone has made this sudden sharing of it
something that needs a little fortification."

18

"We must be early," Sam Otto said, closing the door after he and Basher had come in. "Where is everybody?"

"They'll be along," Devan said, moving two stools out from the wall for them.

"I wouldn't expect them to miss the test," Sam said. Then he brightened. "But getting here early gives me an opportunity to introduce you fellows to Mr. Basher and let you get acquainted with the man who's going to volunteer to go through the Eye tonight."

"You can go straight to hell," Basher said. "I'm volunteering for no Eye duty. Once is enough. I don't want to get stuck in any wilderness again. I only came to watch."

Several others came through the door. Orcutt, tanned, slim and as imposing as ever; Tooksberry, visibly a little older but without the vinegary lines he used to have in his face; Holcombe, who had got over cracking his knuckles and had devoted himself to the manufacture of the camp's wire and who looked much the same; and a youngster Devan recognized as Johnny

Selden, son of one of the foundry workers. He was about sixteen.

"Except for Johnny here," Orcutt said, "this could be ten years ago."

"Let's hope it doesn't end the same way," Basher said.

Devan pushed firmly on the wax fillings in his teeth with his tongue, recalling what lay on the other side of the Eye and hoping at the same time the five men wouldn't be too disconcerted by the knowledge that the Eye would not take them back to Chicago.

He had examined the problem from every angle but always came up with the same answer: he could not tell them before one of them went in and looked around. They had waited, as he had, for ten years to see where the Eye went. He would not have believed Dr. Costigan if the doctor had told him yesterday the Eye did not go back to Chicago; he would have had to see for himself. So he knew he could not tell Orcutt, Basher, Otto, Holcombe or Tooksberry now. They'd have to see for themselves.

"What's the matter with you, Devan?"

Devan started at the mention of his name.

"You look so far away and sad," Orcutt was saying. "Buck up, boy! This is the big night, haven't you heard? This is when we all get a look at Chicago again. It's time for rejoicing. You look as if it were time for a funeral."

"We ought to have a party," Otto said, looking at the doctor. "You have the wherewithal, no doubt."

"No doubt," Dr. Costigan said drily.

"What *is* this?" Orcutt said. "You, Devan, and the doctor—aren't you glad this is the end of the trail, that you'll know?"

"It must be the thought of all this coming to an end," Devan said. "After all, ten years is a long time."

"It is a long time." Orcutt came up and slipped his arm around Devan's shoulder. "Everyone in New Chicago owes a lot to you and the doctor whether the Needle works or not. If we manage to get back to Chicago and civilization with it, all the more credit to you both. We're indebted to you because of your remembrance of so many things and to Dr. Costigan because of his thorough work making it with materials at hand."

"Everyone's worked on it," Devan said.

"Everybody's had a hand in it indirectly," Dr. Costigan said.

"It's what has held us all together, just the same." Orcutt broke away. "Now, is everything set?"

"I'm ready when you are," Dr. Costigan said. "But who is going through?"

"I'm way ahead of you, Doctor." Orcutt put his hand on Johnny Selden's head. The boy blushed.

"You're not going to send a boy through!"

"He has no fillings to lose."

"What do the Seldens think of this, Ed?" Devan asked.

"They put it straight up to Johnny and he said he'd do it. He remembers only vaguely what the real Chicago is like. But he's not going in all the way. Just his head. Are you ready, lad?"

Orcutt escorted the boy to the Eye and Dr. Costigan pulled the switch that energized the Eye area.

"We'll hang on to you, Johnny," Orcutt said. "Just crawl through this opening, just to your shoulders. Leave your hands on this side so you can pull out in case you see anything dangerous."

The boy wet his dry lips, swallowed a couple times and then lay down on the floor, his head toward the Eye. He inched himself forward while Orcutt and Holcombe held one leg and Johnson and Basher held the other.

"Good luck," Sam Otto said.

The boy's head disappeared little by little, first the hair, then the ears and on down his neck to his shoulders. His hands on the sides of the Eye were sweaty and his fingers were rigid. Then the hands relaxed and went to the floor and those who watched him saw, by the different positionings of his body, that he was turning first one way and then another.

"When is he coming out, for heaven's sake?" Holcombe asked.

"He just went in," Dr. Costigan reminded.

Devan imagined what he'd see. Dark sky full of stars and clouds and a moon and wind and stone and grass—unless the weather had changed, if there was weather. It might be raining, or just dark, with no wind and an overcast sky, or a bright, still night with a big moon and memories of a warm day....

The boy finally eased himself out with his hands, rolled over on his back and sat up, blinking his eyes. The men sat around him, curious but patient. Dr.

Costigan turned off the Eye. Devan's nerves tightened for the revelation and its effects.

"Well?" Sam Otto could contain himself no longer.

"I don't know," the boy said.

"What don't you know, son?"

"I don't know what I saw."

"Well, describe it as best you can."

"It's dark—"

Sam groaned.

"—and it's damp—"

"So it's not Chicago after all," Tooksberry said.

"It could be Chicago," Orcutt snapped. "Parts of Chicago are dark and damp. It depends upon where you are."

"But in this section"—Tooksberry pointed through one of the walls—"we're six blocks from where we came through. Six blocks southwest. Where would that be then from where we were? In a forest preserve?"

"No. We'd still be in the industrial district or in the middle of a shopping district," Holcombe said.

"Give the kid a chance to talk," Sam said. "All he's said so far is that it's cold and damp."

"It smells different," Johnny said. "But there was darkness everywhere I looked, though I could feel a breeze in my face."

And Devan thought: I can tell you where you were, kid.

"A sewer," Orcutt said. "It could be a sewer. What a laugh that would be!"

"Is it a bad smell?" Sam asked.

"It's not a good smell."

Devan didn't recall what kind of a smell it was. It hadn't impressed him one way or another.

"Maybe he's in somebody's closet."

"Cellar."

"No breeze there."

"Oh, hell," Orcutt said. "We're getting nowhere. I'm going to take a look and let Dr. Van Ness fill my teeth." Johnny gave him a hurt look, so Orcutt added, "It's not that I doubt your word, young fellow. It's simply that, since you have never lived in the city—at least at a time you can distinctly remember—you are unable to interpret what you see."

"But I didn't see *anything*," the boy protested.

Should I tell them? Devan thought. Before he could decide, Tooksberry was talking.

"What's to be gained by sticking one's head in there if there's nothing to see?" Tooksberry took off his glasses and polished them. "The boy's got eyes, hasn't he?"

Aren't you the smart one! Devan thought.

"It could be Chicago during a blackout," Sam said.

"Another war, Sam? Oh, no!"

"What I mean," Tooksberry said, "is: somebody's got to go in all the way and find out if it is Chicago or not."

Here we go again. Maybe I should have said something.

Basher sighed. "Will someone please show me the way out? This is where I came in."

I don't blame you, Basher.

"Go ahead, Glenn," Orcutt said. "Have your little joke, but Howard's right. It's got to be done. This time, though, there is a place to stand after you go through. That was established with the little Needle. Right, Devan? Dr. Costigan? There's nothing to fear."

Except fear itself. Devan laughed to himself. About time I settled this for them.

"Is there a question in anybody's mind who is going into the Eye this time, then?" Tooksberry smiled as he looked around the group.

"The kid here," Orcutt said, "is the only one of us without fillings in his teeth. But we can't send a boy to do a man's work."

"Is that so?" Tooksberry continued to smile.

"We promised his folks he wouldn't go through all the way," Holcombe said.

Devan felt moved to say something to stop them, but the look on Tooksberry's face stopped him. The man was having a good time if nobody else was. He grinned at them all and then, after having his fill of confounding them with his sudden good nature, he said, "Gentlemen, observe closely, please." With a flourish he extracted both upper and lower plates. "Thimple, ithn't it? No fillingth."

There was some laughter to break the tension.

"We can't let *you* go through, Howard," Orcutt said.

"Why not?"

"It should be someone younger."

"Why? If it'th Chicago, then I will be able to tell quickly. If not, I can tell juth ath quickly and get back here."

"But if it isn't Chicago... If you can't get back..."

Tooksberry was already at the Eye. "Thtart it up, Doctor."

Dr. Costigan looked hard at the man, then looked at the ring of faces, dwelling for a moment on each, a little longer on Devan's. He finally turned and pulled the switch. Devan decided to let the man have a look. There could be no harm. Then they'd all know with certainty.

"Are you sure you want to do this, Howard?"

"We've got to know, Ed." He put his plates on a stool near the Eye, then took off his glasses. "I really don't need glatheth exthept when I read. I'll be able to thee all right." He got down on the floor on his side. "Tell Beatrith..."

His eyes moistened. No one dared look at him.

A moment later there was a slithering noise and he was gone, only his clothes remaining in a little pile in the Eye.

"I hope and pray he comes back," Basher said grimly. "I don't want him going through what I did."

"He'll be all right," Orcutt said.

Devan hoped he'd have sense enough not to move from the ground immediately in front of the Eye. Otherwise he'd probably be gone forever, unless someone went to look for him. It could get terribly involved.

"Howard has certainly changed," Holcombe observed. "He used to be so sour."

Orcutt was filling his pipe. "You've got to give Miss Treat credit for that."

There was no denying that. There wasn't a happier person in the camp than the former Beatrice Treat, a more contented couple than the Tooksberrys. The bitterness, cynicism and disbelief in the man had vanished after his marriage to her and his setting up of the New Chicago Constitution which had been so quickly adopted at a plenary session of New Chicagoans.

Conversation ebbed and flowed as the minutes went by until, after nearly fifteen minutes, they were all silent and jumpy, their eyes on the Needle's Eye. Devan couldn't imagine what the man was doing in the rocky wastes. He had visions of him frantically trying to find the Eye opening so he could return.

It was a full fifteen minutes after that—an agonizing fifteen minutes to every one of them—that a head appeared in the Eye. Devan was glad and breathed a sigh of relief because he had been feeling it was about time for him to stick his head into the Eye and direct the man back to it.

Tooksberry's head had a toothless grin.

"Greetingth," he said. Then he was out and pulling on his clothes.

"Is it Chicago?"

"What did you see?"

"Come on, Howard, don't keep us in suspense."

But Tooksberry wouldn't be hurried, wouldn't say a word until he was fully dressed, his teeth in and his glasses adjusted. Then he eyed them all in turn, enjoying himself. Devan knew what he was going to say but he didn't like the way he was playing it.

But it was Tooksberry's show. Nobody could deny that. And nobody was telling him anything.

"It was Chicago," he said, finally.

Chicago!

Devan sat on his stool in shock, his mouth slack.

The others crowded around the man, eager for details.

Impossible! Devan had been through the Eye and had seen for himself the endless waste of the rocky plain. Why would the man lie? But *was* he lying? The men were still asking questions and Tooksberry was still standing there smiling at them all and not saying anything.

When they had quieted, he said, "It was Chicago. Just as I said. When I first got through the Eye, I found it exactly as Johnny here described it. Damp and dark. Nothing to see. I lay there for a long time trying to figure out where I was, fingering the surface beneath me. I finally concluded it was hard-packed clay from rain that had washed it in where I was, for I could dig down through to an unyielding surface below it.

"I sat up, then stood up. I could feel a breeze, all right. Then my eyes got more accustomed to where I was and I could make out dimly a less dark area in front of me. I wanted to get out of there because I could hear little noises around me and once in a while one of the rats would run over my bare feet. I walked five paces forward and then could see a doorway on my right. I made a right turn and took seven and a half steps to the center of the doorway and then drew my first easy breath because I knew I could get back to the Eye any time I wanted to. All I had to do was locate the doorway.

"On the other side of the doorway it was a little brighter. There were windows without glass in the walls about eye level and I knew it must be in the bottom of a deserted building because I could see the stars through one of the windows and the walls of nearby buildings through the others. At the other end of the basement room there were stairs and I hurried over to these, stepping high over debris and wading through papers and junk. I went up the creaky steps and out into a vacant backyard area and from there around the passageway between two buildings to the street in front of the old place I'd just come out of. I didn't see anyone and was sure no one saw me. If they had, they'd have yelled for a cop, I'm sure.

"Out in front it was much different. Cars whizzed by. I had forgotten they went so fast. And I had forgotten what ten years of progress could do, too. And then, from my place in the shadows, I saw people walking by. I could see their faces in the light of the lamps as they went by. Worried and hungry and tense. Didn't look like us at all. Pale, too. They walked too fast, it seemed to me.

"Then I saw some papers blowing around in the street and I risked showing myself for a moment by reaching out from the passageway and picking up half a page of the Chicago *Tribune*. It was the classified ad section. There was a street light near by, so I leaned out a little bit and read a few of the ads. Same old things. Dishwashers are in great demand. They want people to sell specialties. Just as if it were yesterday, but the date on the newspaper was this morning's.

"I knew I should be getting back, but before I did I ran out to the sidewalk and chanced a look north to the Loop. There was a faint glow of red in the sky, the neon lights. It was Chicago, all right. Cars began slowing down, there were a few cries from people and I knew I had been sighted, so I ran back into the passageway. I would have been here sooner if it hadn't been for the gang of kids coming at me from the back way. I knew there were people behind me as well. I was in a spot."

Tooksberry looked down, knew he had his audience hanging on his every word, looked up and smiled. "I don't have to tell you I made it. I just slid through one of the basement windows. I found the doorway and ducked back here."

Devan could not believe what he had heard, saw that Dr. Costigan was having the same difficulty, raised his eyebrows when their eyes met.

Everyone had been silent for a long time. Then Orcutt got off his stool. "It took a lot of guts to do what you did, Howard. We all appreciate it. Did you tell everything?"

"Everything I remember."

"Did you see what kind of cars they were?" Basher asked. "You mentioned you'd never seen any like them. Can't you describe them?"

"Well, they didn't make the usual car noises. And they seemed a little more low slung and more streamlined. But I never could tell the makes of cars."

"How about styles?" Orcutt asked. "Have they changed?"

"No, I don't think they have, but to be frank, Ed, I can't remember what they were like before, can you?"

Orcutt scratched his head. "The hem line's been up and down so much it's hard to remember where it was at the time of transition."

"Well," Sam Otto said, "all we have to do now is turn on the Needle and let everybody go through."

"It has all been arranged," Orcutt said, looking carefully at Tooksberry. "The council has already decided what should happen in this eventuality. Tomorrow at ten o'clock in the morning there will be a mass meeting of all the residents of New Chicago at this site. At that time we will set up the system of drawing numbers for who is to be first, second and so on, with a man drawing a number for his whole family so they can all crawl through together."

"I need a drink," Dr. Costigan said. "It so happens I have just enough glasses."

"Does it so happen you have anything to put in them?" Sam Otto asked.

"It is time for a drink, all right," Basher said. "We've finally done it. We can finally go back."

"How are you going to let the people know, Ed?" Holcombe asked.

"That's up to Johnson, Jim. He and his men can call on everyone and explain. They have lists and the route to do it in the shortest time. Everything's been thought out, you see. We've discussed it fully with him. He'll do it beginning early in the morning."

The wine was quietly poured and for a while no one had anything to say, which Devan thought odd, considering the occasion. They should have been happy and gay, but he presumed the gravity of the situation made them thoughtful. After all, any great change gives one pause.

"It's going to be different," Otto said soberly, "this getting back to Chicago. I wonder if my friends have missed me."

"It *will* seem strange," Holcombe said.

"We've enjoyed it here, you know?" Tooksberry said. "I don't know why, but I've really found happiness, I think."

"I'm going to miss good old New Chicago," Basher said.

Orcutt raised his glass high. "Here's to New Chicago." Glasses clinked and their contents were drained.

"Is it all right for me to tell my folks about this?" Johnny asked. "They'll want to know."

"You can tell them," Orcutt said.

The boy hurried out. He was later followed by the others until only Dr. Costigan, Orcutt, Devan and Tooksberry were left.

Finally, Tooksberry yawned, stood up and stretched. "I've got to go," he said. "Big day tomorrow, you know."

"So long, Howard," Orcutt said. "See you bright and early. I'll be going soon."

"Mind if I walk with you?" Devan said, leaving Orcutt and the doctor. Tooksberry shook his head and together they walked out into the now cool night. They could faintly hear the waves lapping against the shore as they walked away from the beach and the sandy knoll.

After they had gone part of the way to the enclosure in silence, Devan said, "I've got something to tell you, Howard."

"What is it?" Tooksberry looked at him obliquely as they went down the path.

"I went through the Eye last night."

"Really?" He did not falter in his steps.

"I saw only a rocky plain, a place where outcropping rock was visible for as far as the eye could see. And grass grew out of little crannies and that's the only living thing I saw."

"Depressing sight, the way you describe it."

"Didn't you see the same thing, then?"

"I won't tell anyone you went through the Eye, Dev."

"Why did you tell them it's Chicago?"

Tooksberry stopped and turned to him, the bright moon a bright white dot in either eye. He smiled. "Why didn't you tell them it's not, Devan?"

"You *did* see the same thing as I, then?"

"It's Chicago, all right," Tooksberry said. "It has got to be Chicago. You have to believe that, Dev."

19

One of Johnson's men awakened Devan early with an urgent pounding on the open front door to tell them of the ten o'clock gathering at the Needle site.

"Begging your pardon, Mr. Traylor," he said when Devan approached the front door in his pajamas. Betty, whom he had left asleep, was right behind him. "We have to call on every house. You understand."

"Of course."

"You've told Mrs. Traylor?"

"Not yet." When the policeman gave no evidence he was departing at once, Devan added, "But I will."

The man offered his thanks and was gone.

When Devan had come home the night before, he had been determined to tell her the truth. But the more he thought it over, wondering what Tooksberry meant and why he acted so mysteriously, he became convinced he ought to play along with the man. If the camp knew there was no way back to Chicago, it would be thrown into an uproar. He knew that. But wouldn't it be worse to get all the people down there expecting to go back to Chicago and then to have to tell them that they could never go back?

He hoped Tooksberry knew what he was doing. He realized it was a dangerous thing, this pretending to believe in Chicago, but some compunction made him respect Tooksberry's request. When he explained things to Betty, he did not tell her there was no way back.

Betty's face was white nonetheless as she prepared breakfast.

Devan presumed his own face lacked color. He knew one thing: he could not think straight because his mind was so obsessed with thoughts of the Needle, the people, Chicago, Tooksberry and whether or not he should have told Betty the truth. The result was that his breakfast lay like a heavy ball in his stomach.

When he was ready to go down to the Needle, he said as casually as he could, "I've got to go now. You'll be down?"

She came with him to the door. Her eyes were tear-rimmed. "I'll be there with the children."

He kissed her lightly. She clung to him.

"Devan."

"Yes?"

"Devan." She would not let him go. "Devan"—and the words came now quickly—"we've been so happy together."

The muscle that was his heart had a spasm of gladness that must have sent some oxygen-rich blood to his head because he felt intoxicated, dizzy for a moment.

"I know," he managed to say.

"And Devan..." Her arms were still around him, her lips at his ear. "Devan, let's not stop being happy.

Let's—let's not go back. Don't you see I don't want to go back? Do you?"

He held her tightly, joyously.

"I don't want to go back, Betty." It was amazing how simple it was to say a truth he had denied so long. "I guess I've never really wanted to go back."

She held him at arm's length and looked at him, her face radiant. "Even if we're the only two-four: you and I and the children."

"We'll always be together," he said. "In New Chicago."

The morning was cool and the sun was bright. The lake was complementary to the sky and sun flashes danced on the waves which moved on the shore like armies.

There would have been swimmers if it had not been that they had something else to do this morning. And children, who usually danced and played on the long stretch of beach, were absent. Everyone was either at the building on the dune or was making preparations to go there.

Several long tables had been placed together in front of the door to the Needle building and people came singly, in pairs and in whole families, bringing nothing with them because they knew they would not take anything along on the trip through the Eye.

Orcutt was there stirring the big glass bowl of numbers with a long, wooden cooking spoon and there was a crowd watching. Devan was helping Johnson with the long list of people—there were exactly five hundred and thirty-one, including the newest one born in the hospital early that morning. They were going to have to account for every one; it would not be fair to leave anyone uninformed. Johnson said his men had been to every house in the settlement, that there were only a few absentees: men off hunting somewhere, a couple others who had been gone a month on a tour of exploration.

Devan heard men talking. How were the people in the hospital going to go through the Needle? They would go later and therefore someone would have to remain for a short time, Orcutt explained. There were people out exploring, too, he understood, and something would have to be done about them. But Devan's mind was not on what was being said there. His mind was on what Betty had said. It dwelt on the fact that she had wanted to stay even though she thought she could go back to Chicago. It made his heart sing. It gave him a freedom of thought and expression and feeling he hadn't had for years and it was then that he realized for the first time that the Needle, instead of being a blessing as far as he and Betty were concerned, had stood in the way of their complete happiness.

For reasons that even those who have the feeling are unable to discover, Devan felt that Betty was in the mass of people on the inland slope, turned and found her looking at him. He waved and she and the children and some of his friends near by waved in return. His gladness at staying was only lessened by the thought that all the faces he saw before him wore the expression of people who thought they were going back home. What was going to happen when they found out there was no Chicago to anticipate?

"Devan." He looked up to find Dr. Costigan at his elbow. "About Tooksberry," he began, trying to keep others from hearing.

Devan smiled and said, "Later, Doctor."

"But you know he couldn't have..."

Devan nodded. "I understand, Doctor."

"Ladies and gentlemen of New Chicago." Orcutt was on one of the picnic-type tables, facing the crowd as he had ten years before. "And the kids, too." There was a little laughter. Orcutt looked good, Devan thought. He had the audience waiting on every word. He was a magnetic man, no denying that. Would his magnetic personality be enough to hold and master the crowd when it discovered what he would be saying was a lie?

"The day you have been waiting ten years for is here at last," Orcutt said. "We've gone without a lot of things to build this Needle. Devan Traylor here—stand up, Devan, and let them all have a look at you—and Dr. Winfield Costigan, come on Doc, show them what, as if anybody doesn't know, you look like—have spared no time (I can't say expense because we don't have money here) to perfect this device.

"Last night your representatives met here in the Needle building and Howard Tooksberry—has anyone seen Howard? Yes, there he is—went into the Eye and walked the streets of Chicago for a few minutes. He doesn't have a glowing account because it was at night, but he says it's Chicago, all right, and he read a little in the Chicago *Tribune* to prove it. He wanted to bring it back with him, but he couldn't of course.

"Some time ago the council, knowing that the Needle was nearly completed, worked on the problem of who should be permitted to go back first. I think everybody will agree we can't all make a rush for the Eye. There was to be an efficient system established. So, remembering the days of the draft, we have set up on the table here a glass bowl in which we have deposited a number of slips of paper with numbers on them, ranging from one to two hundred and fifty, the idea being that a man who draws a number takes himself only if he is single, or himself and his entire family, if he has a family.

"We're all set to go and you can come up one at a time and pick your slips and then walk away and make room so others can come up. We don't want any crowding. Now, are there any questions?"

A hand shot up. It belonged to Gus Nelson.

"Yes, Gus?"

"Mr. Orcutt," Nelson said, "can the person who pulls number one just walk right into the Eye or does he have to wait until all the numbers are drawn?"

"He has to wait, Gus. We'll start the parade through the Eye as soon as all the slips are drawn and everyone knows where he is in the big line. It shouldn't take long for everyone to go through. Any other questions?"

"How did it look when Tooksberry went through?" a man in the crowd wanted to know.

"Howard says it looks pretty much as Chicago always did," Orcutt said.

"That's what I was afraid of," the man said.

People laughed.

"All right," Orcutt said. "We're all ready. I'm going to step down now. You folks just come up and get your numbers and then find yourselves your right place in the line."

He stepped down and gave a final swirl of the slips with the wooden spoon.

Nothing much can happen yet, Devan said to himself. Wait until they all get their slips and find out there's no Chicago!

Orcutt put the wooden spoon down slowly, looked at the people in wonderment.

No one stepped forward.

People were looking at each other in surprise.

Orcutt went back to the top of the table. "Didn't you all hear me right? You can get your slips now for the Needle's Eye. You can go back to Chicago. Don't you understand?"

The people were smiling now and some were laughing.

"Gus!" Orcutt said. "Gus Nelson. You asked about whether or not you can walk into the Eye right away. Don't you want a slip?"

Nelson shook his head. "I don't want a slip, Mr. Orcutt. I just wondered what happened to the person who pulled number one. I knew I wouldn't pick it because I'm not going to pull any out. I'm staying here."

"You're staying? Why?"

"I've got my work. Making steel is pretty important and I have a special high-grade type of carbon steel I'm working on right now and it's got another day to go in the charcoal. I couldn't leave before then, anyway." He smiled rather sheepishly. "Besides, there's a girl—a woman. She and I talked about staying and we don't care what the rest do. We're staying."

First a few giggles rippled through the crowd. Then there was scattered applause and this became stronger, increasing until it seemed everybody was clapping. Then it tapered off.

"I can tell you why *I'm* not going," a voice came across the crowd from the outside fringe. It was Dr. Van Ness. Everybody turned to look at him. "Back in Chicago I'd have no practice. Too old. I'm over sixty-five and people used to say, 'Why don't you retire and give some young fellow a chance?' Even my colleagues said that. Well, I did. I retired and I was unhappy. I developed so many aches and pains life was just plain miserable.

"That's the way it was until I came to New Chicago. Here I was wanted and here I want to stay. I want to die here, not in Chicago. I've been so busy putting in fillings the way they ought to be put in I've had no chance to think about anything else. I make every one of them a work of art and I'm proud of them and I hate to think of all those fine fillings dropping out as everyone goes through the Needle. And another thing: I've got three young assistants and they're doing a fine job. I hope they stay with me and I think they will. We'll take care of the teeth of anybody who stays. And, as in the past, it won't cost you a cent."

"If you think I'm going to walk along dirty old Chicago streets again, you're mad." It was Mrs. Petrie. "All I used to do is knit and listen to the radio and attend board of directors meetings. You know about that,

Mr. Orcutt. I never had anything interesting happen to me before I came through the Eye. And I have had fun working here with the looms, making the cloth your suits are made of. I couldn't be going now, anyway. I've got a new design worked out on the loom and it will take me all day to do that. Besides, I've got lots of other designs to work out. I just can't keep up with them. Anybody who thinks I'm going to give all that up for knitting and radio is crazy."

There was a deafening applause. Devan was profoundly moved. There was a lump in his throat and there were tears in his eyes and smiles on the faces of people around him. He got to the top of the table and looked out over the people and saw Betty and she saw him and they laughed and waved.

A man jumped upon the table, held his arms aloft for silence. "Most of you know me," he said, when they had quieted. "My name's Elmo Hodge. If you don't know me too well it's because I've been so busy building telescopes and making star maps. Beats the grocery business all to hell."

When they laughed he held his hands high again. "There are faces in the crowd I recognize as belonging to people who owe me money. They had run up bills at my store. We were living in an awful inflationary time, remember?" More laughter. They remembered. "Well, it's not just because I like telescopes better that I'm staying. Not just. I'll tell you why. I just got awful tired of making out reports in duplicate and triplicate and quintuplicate. It got so I was spending more time making out reports for the state and national governments than I was waiting on my customers. I had to hire an extra bookkeeper to help me out. Do I want to go back to that? I'll let you folks answer for me."

The crowd yelled "No!" while Hodge jumped off the table platform. Somebody yelled a solo that could be heard above the general noise, "Not only 'No!' but 'Hell, no!'"

Orcutt spied Eric Sudduth. "How about you, Eric? Don't you want to go back?"

"Haven't finished my work here," he said. "Got the Bible almost all done. Just a few places missing and I'll think of those and others I'm sure will help. But I'll never have time to finish it if I go back."

"We don't need the Needle!" someone yelled.

"Without the Needle we can make other things."

"Let's use the Needle parts for what we need."

"Tear it down!"

"Push it over!"

"Let's burn it!"

Orcutt's voice bellowed out over the clamor. His arms beat the air in a command for silence and, after a while, he got it.

"No," he said. "We won't wreck it. We need parts from it too much to do that. We'll take it apart piece by piece and use the pieces. Well have some things we've been holding back on now. Our own radio station, an airplane perhaps. We'll never need automobiles. We have a lot of exploring to do, do you people realize that? Now without the Needle to think about we can start finding out what kind of a world this is we find ourselves in. We've got map-making and charting to do—we have a world here we can make whatever we want it to be. We can start all over again and make it the way we want it, the way it ought to be."

Dr. Costigan brought out bottles of wine and set them on the table and from somewhere produced a number of glasses. People, the tension over, without the Needle to worry about, with no Chicago as an eventuality, talked gaily and happily and made plans for the coming years.

The men laughed and spun yarns on the golden, sunlighted hill and women visited and children ran over the sand and across the beach.

Once Devan looked at Orcutt and wondered if he knew. But he couldn't have because only Tooksberry, Dr. Costigan and Devan himself knew. And now Devan knew what Tooksberry meant about having faith in Chicago. The people had to deny themselves Chicago, had to denounce it when it was possible. If they had thought it was not so, they would have been unhappy, would have wanted it too much.

"What's the look for, Dev?" Orcutt said, in between sips of wine. "You don't have to answer. I think I know. How can a man leave his reading glasses on one side of the Needle and read the classified ad section of the Chicago *Tribune* on the other side? Is that what you were thinking?"

"Something like that," Devan said.

"It was a terrible spot to be in," Tooksberry said. Beatrice was beside him. "I stood on that rocky plain for a long time. It was quiet and peaceful, though. I'll say that for it. It gave me the time I needed to figure it out. It was the only thing I could do. Don't you believe that?"

"Yes," Devan said. "I believe that. Now."

Betty, who was sitting next to him, squeezed his hand and they watched their children running with others under the late morning sun.

They jerked to attention at shouts from the direction of the lake. Devan thought: Someone has fallen in.

Many people were running to the top of the sand ridge, were running along it, looking at the water. Many were pointing.

Devan looked where they were pointing.

A man was swimming off the shore a hundred feet, his white arms and back a strange sight for bronzed New Chicagoans, and when he came within seventy-five feet of the beach, he found his footing.

The man started to walk out of the water.

He was naked.

He smiled.

He waved to the people on the sand hill.

ABOUT THE AUTHOR

An Introduction to Jerry Sohl

by Jennifer Sohl

 Best known for his scripts for TV series such Star Trek, The Twilight Zone, The Outer Limits, Alfred Hitchcock Presents, and his many movies and novels, my father first sharpened his writing skills in newspapers. He reported news and reviewed drama and music as a freelance writer and photographer for The Daily Pantagraph in Bloomington, Illinois from 1946-1958.

He loved SF and back then he was struggling to find a more creative outlet for his talent. One Evening in 1951 my father interviewed famous Science Fiction writer Wilson (Bob) Tucker for an article about him in the Daily Pantagraph. During the interview my father explained an idea for a book he thought Bob should write.

Bob suggested "You should write the Book, Jerry, being that you know the plot line." (Bob Tucker didn'tt think very highly of Newspaper Reporters. He thought they all were cynical, ego-inflated. cigarette-smoking boozeheads, who hated fiction, especially anything as crazy as Science Fiction or Fantasy.)

So this was a bluff.

After the interview my father went home, and that evening began writing The Haploids.

It was published in 1952 by Rinehart & Co.

And surprised the hell out of Bob Tucker.

That was only the beginning... The Haploids was the first of several novels that marked him as a professional craftsman.

In 1958 we moved to California where my father wanted to break into television. At an SF convention my father met 4 other SF writers, Richard Matheson, Charles Beaumont, Theodore Sturgeon, and George Clayton Johnson. They called themselves The Green Hand (a play on the Black Hand of the Mafia). But the television producers didn't seem to understand what they were pitching, because when ever the producers were visited it was always with one person at a time; so they finally gave up and went their separate ways.

As one biography put it, Jerry Sohl delighted in contributing to viewers' sleepless nights.

The overall feeling he had was that it would have been a mistake for him to do anything else.

In a 1988 interview he said, "Then you have people come up to you and say 'I really loved that novel. It changed my life.' I get so much of that and it is a tremendous feeling of accomplishment. What it all comes down to is that it has all been great fun and should I die in the next minute I don't think I would regret anything I've done."

People are made for what they do—and my father was indeed made for writing. It was the only thing he wanted to do.

ReAnimus Press

Breathing Life into Great Books

If you enjoyed this book we hope you'll tell others or write a review! We also invite you to subscribe to our newsletter to learn about our new releases and join our affiliate program (where you earn 12% of sales you recommend) at www.ReAnimus.com.

Here are more ebooks you'll enjoy from ReAnimus Press, available from ReAnimus Press's web site, Amazon.com, bn.com, etc.:

Costigan s Needle, by Jerry Sohl

Night Slaves, by Jerry Sohl

The Mars Monopoly, by Jerry Sohl

One Against Herculum, by Jerry Sohl

The Time Dissolver, by Jerry Sohl

The Transcendent Man, by Jerry Sohl

I, Aleppo, by Jerry Sohl

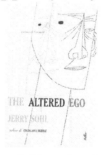

The Altered Ego, by Jerry Sohl

The Anomaly, by Jerry Sohl

Death Sleep, by Jerry Sohl

The Odious Ones, by Jerry Sohl

Point Ultimate, by Jerry Sohl

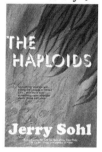

The Haploids, by Jerry Sohl

Prelude to Peril, by Jerry Sohl

The Resurrection of Frank Borchard, by Jerry Sohl

The Lemon Eaters, by Jerry Sohl

The Spun Sugar Hole, by Jerry Sohl

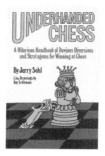

Underhanded Chess, by Jerry Sohl

Underhanded Bridge, by Jerry Sohl

Night Wind, by Roberta Jean Mountjoy

Black Thunder, by Roberta Jean Mountjoy

Dr. Josh, by Jerry Sohl

Blowdry, by Jerry Sohl

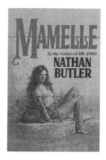

Mamelle, by Jerry Sohl

Kaheesh, by Jerry Sohl

The Exiles Trilogy, by Ben Bova

The Star Conquerors (Standard Edition),
by Ben Bova

Escape!, by Ben Bova

Colony, by Ben Bova

The Kinsman Saga, by Ben Bova

Star Watchmen, by Ben Bova

As on a Darkling Plain, by Ben Bova

The Winds of Altair, by Ben Bova

Test of Fire, by Ben Bova

The Weathermakers, by Ben Bova

The Dueling Machine, by Ben Bova

The Story of Light, by Ben Bova

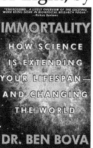

Immortality, by Ben Bova

Space Travel - A Science Fiction Writer's Guide, by Ben Bova

Ghosts of Engines Past, by Sean McMullen

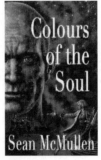

Colours of the Soul, by Sean McMullen

The Cure for Everything, by Severna Park

Bug Jack Barron, by Norman Spinrad

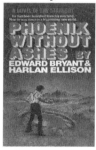

Phoenix Without Ashes, by Harlan Ellison
and Edward Bryant

Particle Theory, by Edward Bryant

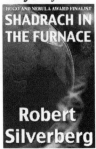

Shadrach in the Furnace, by Robert Silver-

berg

Commencement, by Roby James

Bloom, by Wil McCarthy

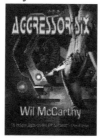

Aggressor Six, by Wil McCarthy

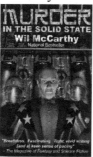

Murder in the Solid State, by Wil McCarthy

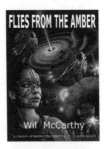

Flies from the Amber, by Wil McCarthy

The Sigil Trilogy (Omnibus vol.1-3), by Henry Gee

"Great stuff... everything you yearn to find in a very good contemporary SF novel. Really enjoyed it!"
--*SFWA Grandmaster* **Michael Moorcock**

"Brisk, funny, triumphant--and utterly compelling."
--*Greg Bear*

Watch for these and many more great titles from Re-Animus Press!

79307072R00177

Made in the USA
Middletown, DE
09 July 2018